Contents

Good Tidings

A Christmas Anthology

The Lady Lits

Edited by Sarah Soon and J. B. Wilson
Cover Design by Mari Eygabroad
Interiors by Susan Graham

For Nancy

Your warm, gentle spirit
and childlike love for Jesus
invited us to follow you
on a journey of
compassion, humility, kindness, and generosity.

We miss you,
but your wisdom and strong presence taught us
we have nothing to fear.

In honor of the gift of your inspiration,
we will strive
to be encouragers
focused on and faithful to
Our Savior.

Foreword

"Are you looking for guests for your podcast?"

Nancy Ness asked me this question in late 2022, introducing me to the amazing Lady Lits.

Formed after participation in a challenge that nurtured community, their writing group had been going strong for over a year. I said yes and, after some thought, decided to interview them as a panel. Already a friend of Nancy and an admirer of Jill and Mari, I delighted in meeting Linda, Susan, Sarah, and Janet.

When preparing for our podcast episode, I heard a Lady Lits Christmas anthology was in the works, and excitement rose up. As the author of a Christmas devotional, I spend more than a few months considering this holiday and keep my eyes open year-round for messages that celebrate the birth of Jesus. I'm pleased to say this beautiful collection of stories ticks every box for me. I laughed out loud, encountered episodes of tingly skin, and leaked a few tears of joy. My favorite aspect of *Good Tidings* is that each story, deeply personal to the authors, captures the spirit of Christmas in a way that honors the Lord. And I cannot wait for my family to create and taste the delectable recipes included.

As I got to know these seven skilled writers, I learned the Bible verse that inspires them is Psalm 45:1: "My heart is stirred by a noble theme as I recite my verses for the king; my tongue is the pen of a skillful writer" (NIV). I believe these Christmas tales were birthed from hearts transformed by truth from Scripture. As you take in their stories, I pray your hearts would experience transformation as well. May the outflow of these recitations to King Jesus, at a time that commemorates his birth, prepare your hearts for Christmas and bless you abundantly.

Jennifer Elwood, author of *Counting Up to Christmas: 24 Gifts from the Gospel of Luke* and host of *The Refuge* podcast.

About the Lady Lits

Who are the Lady Lits? We're glad you asked!

We are a group of writers spread across the United States, Southern Africa, and France. How on earth did we find each other? Through social media, of course.

Two years ago, we were seven writers among many participating in author Ginny L. Yttrup's online group for equipping and encouraging writers. We connected while commenting on a post. Nancy Ness asked if anyone in that discussion wanted to create a group allowing us to support one another, brainstorm ideas, and share writing knowledge. We all responded. Yes, please! And the Lady Lits was born.

We meet over video chat every two weeks, to do all the above. In addition, group members gather online regularly to work side-by-side on individual projects, a great form of motivation and accountability.

Writing is a lonely endeavor made much richer through relationships with other authors. The bonds of friendships the Lady Lits have developed around writing have been invaluable.

Good Tidings: A Christmas Anthology is our first collaborative effort. We hope these holiday tales and tasty treats will bring you warmth and cheer.

Light Shows the Way

by Nancy Ness

DECEMBER 8

Turning off the Pacific Coast Highway, Rooney followed the curves of the two-lane road to the top of the hill. Christmas lights twinkled around the roofline of Roseanna's Café, mirroring the glistening moonlight on the water. *In seven years of marriage, Jack and*

I have never been here together. Why do I feel so sad when I'm the one that left?

She turned onto Lilac Lane and then down the narrow alley. Homes built in the '50s and '60s dotted the steep hillside overlooking the ocean. New street signs accommodated vacation homes that had changed the landscape of the town. Parking in front of the detached garage, Rooney looked at the house her grandparents had lived in for fifty years. *Did I make the right decision to move here?*

The next morning, Rooney parked in front of the secondhand store, the only shop in town with rusty lawn chairs prominently placed near the front door that jingled when she opened it.

"With you in a minute," hollered a voice from the back.

Walking down each aisle, Rooney noticed the old pieces and wondered about their history. A vintage dressing table stood in the shadow of a highboy dresser. Rooney tucked a long, chestnut curl behind her ear. She ran her slender fingers over the table's scalloped Bakelite drawer pulls, then along the darkened strip on its top where the mirror had been.

"Can I help you?"

Rooney breathed in the homey scent of linseed oil. She squinted and tilted her head. "Is there a mirror?"

The salesman shook his head. "It's probably hanging on the wall of a remodeled powder room somewhere."

Rooney glanced at him. "I'll take it."

"Without the mirror?"

"Yes." Rooney pulled out the top drawer where Mom's brush would've been. "My mom had one like this."

Mom had sat on a small bench in front of hers, brushing her long chestnut hair. She'd look in the mirror and see Rooney. Then she'd brush Rooney's hair, slowly. Watching each other, they'd let their heads touch. From the doorway, Dad would say, "I can't tell where one chestnut mane stops and the other starts."

Their home in Spokane was sold the summer before Rooney went to college. *Where did the dressing table go?*

She handed her money and keys to the young man. As he loaded her purchase into the back of her Honda, she stopped at the shelves lined with books. A blue-and-white cover caught her eye. Flipping through the wrinkled mimeographed pages of a church cookbook, Rooney chuckled at the note "Magic on a plate!" scribbled in the margin next to "Sylvia's Lemon Pound Cake." The book opened to a page marked by a yellowed recipe card labeled "Tender Crisp Sugar Cookies."

Gran always had a tin of sugar cookies waiting when Rooney and her parents visited at Christmas. *Until that Christmas.* Rooney breathed in and out. *I didn't know it would be the last with Mom and Dad.* She placed a ten-dollar bill near the register and put the cookbook and recipe card in her bag.

Returning home, Rooney parked at the back of the house and walked to the end of the alley. Several locals looked through binoculars toward the ocean. A man wearing an orange knit beanie clutched a coffee mug in his hands. "The grays are back."

Rooney smiled. A woman in a navy-and-white parka, shorts, and flip-flops handed Rooney her binoculars. "Look in front of the twin rocks."

After a few minutes, Rooney saw a spout and a flick of a tail as the whale submerged. She shook her head slowly. "So amazing. I never get tired of seeing this. They stop here to feed, right?" She handed back the binoculars.

The woman nodded. "This is the best time to see them now that its winter."

Rooney glanced at the midcentury modern house to her left. An older man stood on the deck with binoculars. *Grandpa and I used to stand there with him and scan the water looking for spouts. I can't believe Mr. Hein still lives here.*

She reached the bottom of the hill. A chalkboard sign in front of the coffee shop showed the morning and evening times for low and high tide, along with the reminder "Never turn your back on the ocean."

Opening the door, she paused to take in racks of colorful surfboards and wet suits hanging on the wall to the left. The smell of fresh brew lured her to the right. "Tall Americano with cream, please. For here."

The barista gave Rooney her change. "Are you visiting for Christmas?"

She shook her head. "I moved into my grandparents' home on Lilac."

"Welcome to our little piece of heaven."

From a barstool near the window, Rooney savored the warmth of her coffee and the freedom of having nowhere to go. *I could be stuck in a high-rise office building, only dreaming of being here.* The passion she once felt for her work, designing sportswear for Swimmana, had been replaced with the pressure of profit margins.

Jack and I spent so much time together after college, traveling and working remotely. Bend offered employment and the best skiing and white water rafting in Oregon, right out our back door. I fell in love with the Cascades and the Deschutes River. I thought he did too.

Rooney took the last sip of her coffee. The morning clouds had rolled inland, and the sky above the horizon was now clear. *We haven't skied or even gone to the river together in two years.*

She left her mug near the cash register.

As she walked back up the hill, Mr. Hein wrestled his garbage bin down his driveway. Rooney reached him just as he tilted the bin upright. "Looks like you got it."

"Yes, thanks."

In his black-rimmed glasses, he looked like an aging Gregory Peck. Rooney stuck out her hand. "Mr. Hein, I'm Rooney."

"I remember."

She glanced across the yard. "Gran and I would stop at the corner and watch the deer eat apples under the old tree."

"There aren't as many deer now. Trees were cut down to make room for vacation homes. So many things have changed."

Rooney nodded.

"Families used to move in and never leave. Now, they come for just a few weeks in summer." Mr. Hein shook his head.

Rooney took a step forward. "The hillside has changed, but it still has that small-town feel."

"Once we saw what was happening, the locals met at Roseanna's to come up with a plan. The city ordinances were amended to limit new construction."

"Well, you still have the best view in town. I remember gorgeous sunsets and whale watching from your deck. I need to find the binoculars Grandpa gave me."

"When you do, come back and have tea."

"I'd like that." Rooney turned toward home. "It's a date."

That evening, she took her plate to the table. Her phone rang just as she stabbed the last brussels sprout with her fork. *Jack.*

She put her dishes in the sink. The stars were brilliant against the dark sky. "Why is he calling?"

Sitting on the couch, she pushed the button for voice mail. "I just wanted to see if you were okay." His voice seemed far away.

Rooney leaned back and dangled her legs over the couch's arm. *Why did he call? I don't know what to say to him. I don't even know what to feel.*

She pulled the quilt from the back of the couch over her arms, then closed her eyes against tears.

Placing the last of the clean dishes in the cupboard, Rooney laid the dish towel over the sink to dry and touched the canvas hanging on the pantry door. The Bible verse on the canvas was neatly lettered.

"Fear not, I have called you and know you by name." Isaiah 43. I must have read this a hundred times.

Sadness tugged at her like a heavy winter coat. She looked around the kitchen. *When did I start doubting that God saw me, that I didn't have to be afraid? Was it when Mom and Dad died?*

Rooney straightened the placemats on the kitchen table and picked up the yellowed recipe card. "No name."

She read the handwriting on the back out loud. "Every December 13, my grandmother and I made angel cookies to celebrate the Festival of Lights in honor of Santa Lucia. According to Scandinavian Christmas lore, Santa Lucia wore a head wreath made of laurel and adorned with candles. The lights on her head wreath helped guide persecuted Christians hiding in tunnels. I still use the cookie cutter my great-grandmother used."

The loop of each cursive *l* was identical to the last.

Zipping on her coat, Rooney headed out the door and down the alley. Mr. Hein's mailbox was open. She retrieved his mail just as he came through his front gate. "Mr. Hein, I hope you don't mind. I was walking this way."

"Lewis. You can call me Lew." He smiled as he took his mail. "I just put the kettle on."

Lew carried a tray into the family room, where they sat in cream-colored leather chairs near the window facing the ocean.

He took a sip of tea. "So, Ed and Eloise's house. What brings you back here?"

Rooney rested her elbow on the arm of the chair. "Change." She sighed. "A change of pace. Everyone thought I was crazy to leave my dream job."

Lew waited.

"Jack and I are struggling. He seems to thrive in the world of big money and real estate deals. To him, tiny beachside communities are where you go to retire."

Rooney stirred her tea. "I couldn't stay in the city and watch our marriage slip away. This is the place where I was happy, with my parents and grandparents. Walking the beach and whale watching with Grandpa. Baking in the kitchen with Gran, my parents outside in aluminum folding chairs passing the binoculars back and forth. It was always cold in December, but they shared a wool blanket and a plaid thermos of coffee between them."

Lew nodded. "Some things do stay the same." He put his cup on the end table and laced his hands together. "You were a teenager when you lost your parents?"

Rooney frowned. "Seventeen."

"How does someone so young get over that?"

There was kindness in the way he said it. She drew a breath in. "I don't know that I have." Rooney looked down.

"I'm so sorry that happened." He cleared his throat. "I remember Eloise stayed with you in Spokane so you could finish high school there."

"They tried to make things normal for me. Then I went to the college my parents and I chose, just like we planned. Jack and I met in Freshmen English."

They watched the clouds roll inland and the sky above the ocean clear.

Lew topped off his tea and poured more for Rooney. "Nancy Karlsson was seventeen when we met. She was the love of my life. Fifty-three years of marriage, all in this house."

"That's unheard of."

Lew chuckled. "What? A long marriage or staying put in one place?"

"Both, really."

"Nancy taught me the secret to a long marriage. She was intentional about everything. When she got sick, she gave our housekeeper, Stella, explicit instructions to keep the kitchen stocked with my favorite tea, green olives, rye bread, and that thinly sliced ham."

Rooney smiled. "I wish I'd known Nancy better. How did you deal with losing her?"

Lew peered into his cup as if Earl Gray had the answer. "Instead of hiding from grief, I stared back at it. That winter was the coldest on record. It even snowed on New Year's Day."

Rooney leaned forward on the arm of the chair.

"The colder and nastier it was outside, the more I bellowed. You have to acknowledge grief to get past it. Now I open the window at night and let the waves and memories of our life together croon me to sleep."

Lew lifted his glasses and wiped his eyes with his finger. There was silence between them as they watched the sliver of sun melt into the horizon.

"I should go now." Rooney took the tray to the kitchen. She zipped her jacket up to her chin. "Thank you for the tea." She touched Lew's arm. "And the conversation."

Lew held the door open. "Until next time."

At the end of the driveway, she looked back. Lew already seemed like an old friend.

ROONEY MADE THREE DOZEN angel cookies, one dozen for the freezer. Piping miniature green leaves for a laurel wreath on each angel head, she added six tiny frosting stars to represent candlelight. She placed the cookies in a box lined with parchment paper and put on her coat.

The glow of twinkling lights from the tree in Lew's living room lit the driveway. He opened the door and Christmas lyrics floated from the stereo. They reminded Rooney of Christmas Eve candlelight services her family attended in the little white church near the highway.

In the living room, Rooney opened the box of cookies, and their sugar crystals glistened under the lights of the tree. Lew bit into a soft cookie with a chewy outside. "Nancy made sugar cookies every year, on December 13. If she was here now, she would ask you for your recipe."

He opened the lid of a box on the table. "Do you know the story of Santa Lucia?"

Rooney tilted her head and put her hand to her mouth.

Lew picked up the worn gold ribbon and placed the angel on the tree.

Handwritten inside the lid was the story of Santa Lucia, the loop in each *l* exactly like the last one. Rooney touched Lew's arm. "I'll be right back."

She ran down his driveway, up the hill to the alley, and inside her grandparents' house. The recipe card was on the kitchen counter. She ran back to Lew's and let herself in the front door.

"This recipe card was stuck inside a cookbook I found at the secondhand store."

Lew held the card. He drew a sharp breath and exhaled slowly. "I'd recognize her writing anywhere."

Tears welled up in his eyes. He held the card closer and chuckled. "I can smell the vanilla. She must have let someone borrow it. I thought I'd never see it again."

He swallowed hard and handed the card back to Rooney. "This was meant for you."

Rooney blinked back tears. "Thank you," she whispered.

They sat down with glasses Lew filled with eggnog.

"Jack called." She looked at Lew. "I didn't answer."

He leaned forward. "Did you return his call?"

Rooney bit her lower lip. "I couldn't."

He nodded. "Do you know why?"

"I don't know what to say to make things right between us."

She sat back in the chair. "Why did he call? Does he finally want to experience everything lovely about this tiny seaside town that has meant so much to me? What if he does come and nothing has changed?"

Lew shifted in his chair. "There's one way to find out."

Rooney hesitated. "What if . . . What if I refuse to go home with him and this time he is gone forever?"

She sighed and rubbed her eyes. "Do you believe God sees each of us? That he cares if Rooney in Oregon is happy?"

He nodded. "Yes. God uses people and circumstances to guide us. There's a verse in my favorite book, the book of Job." Lew gave a sideways smile. "Not everyone's favorite, I know. It says God sees the ends of the earth and everything under the heavens. And then there's a verse from 2 Chronicles, a truth I've leaned on over the years—'For the eyes of the Lord range throughout the earth to strengthen those whose hearts are fully committed to him.'"

Rooney stopped at the bottom of Lew's driveway. The sky was a canopy of inky black, dotted with pinholes of light. *God placed the stars in the night sky and knows me by name.* She brushed a tear from her cheek.

At home, Rooney hung up her coat and walked down the hall to her grandparents' office. From the desk, she picked up the framed photograph of her mother and dad taken on their fifteenth wedding anniversary. She smiled remembering her dad's chuckle that often ended in a snort. Tracing the outline of her mother's face, her voice caught. "We never got to say goodbye."

Rooney opened the large lower drawer, looking for the binoculars. She pulled out a stack of what looked like magazines. *Calendars?* She brought the stack to the kitchen.

Pink dogwood bloomed on the front of 2012. She flipped through the pages, and a day in December caught her eye. "Gin rummy at Nancy's. Ate Christmas cookies and watched *ATWT*." Gran had written on the free calendars from Tillamook Milk like they were journals.

Over dinner, Rooney continued reading. Nancy and Gran watched *Lucy* reruns and stumbled over the lyrics of Perry Como's greatest hits. As Gran's condition worsened, Nancy coordinated visits with people from church, and every calendar square was covered. Nancy's friendship sustained Gran during the last months of her life.

It is my turn to be a friend to Lew.

After changing into her old jeans and tennis shoes, Rooney used a dolly to unload the dressing table into the garage. It took over an hour to scrub decades of grime from the piece. Wearing a dust mask and gloves, she rubbed the dark walnut surface with a superfine sanding sponge and then wiped it with a damp cloth. Rooney gave herself permission to feel sad. She wiped her nose on her sleeve.

It was almost midnight when she finished cleaning up. She stopped at the garage door and admired her work. "Mom would have loved this."

Dreamy, sea-blue chalk paint had given the piece new life. Something welled up inside Rooney, gratitude mixed with the pain of missing those she loved the most.

In the living room, Rooney cranked the window out and locked it open.

Lew stared back at grief and faced it head-on.

On the corner of the couch, she pulled Gran's quilt over her. "God, show me the way."

Rooney stifled a sob, not wanting to cry, but the exhaustion of pretending everything was okay had become too much. She leaned her head against the back of the couch and her breathing matched the ebb and flow of the waves. Rooney's heart opened and tears flowed easily, bottled-up tears that she had pushed down for too long. Her body heaved as tears fell down her face. She slid onto the cushions and pulled her knees up to her chest. Wiping her face with the corner of the blanket, Rooney closed her eyes. Waves rushed to the shore and roared back again.

The house was cold when she woke, and she got up to close the window.

Picking up her phone, she pushed the green Call button. Jack answered on the first ring.

"Rooney, I'm glad you called. I've been thinking . . ."

Is it over? "What have you been thinking?"

"About you. My visit to Oceanside is long past due. I want to see you."

Rooney put her hand on her knee to stop both from shaking. "Okay. What about Christmas Eve?"

"Yeah. Or this weekend?"

Rooney took a breath in. "You bring the Cab, and I'll make a trip to town for Wagyu rib eye. But bring enough for three. I think you'll like our dinner guest; he reminds me of you in forty years."

"Deal. One more thing. Are dogs allowed in your grandparents' house?"

"Yes, always."

Rooney smiled after they said goodbye. *It would be fun to run with a dog on the beach.*

She laid back on the couch and pulled the quilt up to her chin. *Would I have called Jack if it wasn't for Lew?*

Through the window, Rooney could see the light from the Christmas star at the peak of Lew's roof. It made a soft, round glow in the cold ocean air.

"God lights the way."

Story Inspiration

I RECEIVED INSPIRATION FOR Rooney's story during a summer stay in the tiny beachside community of Oceanside, Oregon. In a rented house on a hillside overlooking the ocean, I climbed the narrow staircase to the tiny upstairs bedroom. Unlatching the small window, I pushed it out and locked it open. Ocean waves lulled me to sleep.

Decorating angel cookies in honor of Santa Lucia is a Nordic custom familiar to me from childhood because my grandparents immigrated to Washington State from Norway. Grandma Darling passed the sugar cookie recipe to my mother and then to me. I bake this cookie recipe with my daughters and granddaughters every Christmas.

I'm donating my proceeds from this anthology to Samaritan's Purse (samaritanspurse.org).

About Nancy

WHEN NANCY NESS RECENTLY found a journal she kept as a teenager, she smiled rereading the entry "Ten Things to Do before I Get Old." Writing a book was at the top of the list. Joining the Lady Lits compelled Nancy to begin writing her first historical fiction novel. Set in the early 1900s, its story is inspired by her grandmother's experience of abandonment and search for family truth.

Nancy passed away unexpectedly in July 2023. Her compassionate storytelling and steady encouragement for others are deeply missed. She was a member of Compel Training, Oregon Christian Writers, and Bible Study Fellowship. Sunday family dinners filled her with joy, and she considered her most important work to be pouring into her family to leave a legacy of love.

She was working toward the publication of a nonfiction book that shares how the words God speaks through Scripture laid the foundation for her emotional healing from abuse. That book will be finalized and published by her daughters. Through her writing, Nancy excelled at her passion to help others discover their own paths to healing.

Lina's Choice

by Sarah Soon

DECEMBER 16—ROHLICKY DAY 1

Lina folded the concert flyer and placed it face down on the kitchen table. It was 9:45 a.m., and if she wasn't at her mom's by ten o'clock sharp, she'd get the privilege of hearing a lecture on the social consequences of tardiness.

At 10:05, she found her mother standing in front of a copper bowl. Her light blue seersucker apron, slightly fringed and faded, looked almost gray. Wearing it was her way of honoring Babi, Lina's great-grandma. Lina didn't oppose her mom's loyalty to Babi, just how rigidly her mom upheld a generation of traditions, acting as though not following them to the letter could cause their family to fall apart.

"You're late," her mom said, frowning as she vigorously whisked egg yolks by hand.

A Burl Ives Christmas record spun on the cherrywood turntable her mom brought out every holiday. Lina preferred more contemporary music, but she hoped the throwback tunes could inject joy, especially on a dreary day. The clouds were gray and imposing, as the morning's light barely illuminated through the patio glass door off the kitchen.

"Sorry, but I lost track of time talking on the phone with Grands." Lina set her purse on the kitchen table. "You didn't tell me she wasn't coming today to help prepare the rohlicky." She scowled as vanilla from a candle set on the table wafted up her nose. Of all the myriad of holiday aromas available, her mom never altered from vanilla.

"Grands doesn't need to be on her feet for two days, especially with the party."

Lina shot her mom a cold look for usually assuming she knew what everyone needed. "Let Grands make that decision."

"You'll have all day with her tomorrow."

"But I always make rohlicky on both days with her. It's tradition. It gets old when you override everything."

"I interfered because you don't think things through but run headlong toward whatever suits your fancy."

Lina opened her mouth, but her mom spoke first. "Before you argue, your tardiness reflects how self-absorbed you can be. Your *dis-*

respect gets old." Her mom whisked harder. "Anyway, we don't have time to waste. Start making the yeast."

"Fine." Lina touched her cross necklace as her vow to get along with her mom echoed in her mind. Earlier that morning, a proverb from her daily devotional had pricked her heart. It said a father's wisdom and a mother's instructions were a crown of grace and a necklace of honor. Why did God make Lina so different from her mom? They struggled to find common ground outside of their love for plants and flowers.

Her mom hummed along with the record. The lyrics about sweet surprises ushered Lina's focus to the pastries. She added warm water to the bowl of yeast and sugar and whisked lightly with a fork.

The music stopped. "Have you decided what you're wearing tomorrow?" Her mom's tone softened.

Lina's eyes brightened. When she spotted a Christmas skirt at the local boutique last week, she dashed to the rack and tried it on in the dressing room. It contoured to her small waist perfectly, as though custom-made for her. "A skirt and a soft, cream *cashmere* sweater." With her mom's preferences in mind, she lingered on the word *cashmere* as long as she could.

"A new outfit?" Her mom's tone, slightly high-pitched, indicated she was working hard to sound congenial. *Maybe Mom also vowed to get along.*

"Yes, for Christmas." Lina flashed a smile.

"What color?"

As Lina approached her mom, Chanel No. 5 wafted up between them. Lina recalled the same scent enveloping her many times as a girl standing in her mother's closet, swaying awkwardly to find her balance as she tried on her mom's heels.

Now, she leaned close to her mother's shoulder and lifted her phone toward her mom's face. "See?"

In the pic, Lina stood in front of a mirror, donning the outfit for the party. The sweater came to her waist, meeting a mint-green skater skirt with rows of Christmas trees on the bottom and 3-D snowflakes embroidered throughout.

Her mother pushed the phone away. "Is this a joke?"

Lina set her phone on the counter, desperate to defend her choice while appeasing her mom. "Think of the skirt as representing a kroj." *Good one.* She enjoyed donning the traditional garb at the annual Czech and Slovak festival downstate.

"Don't insult our ancestors. That's nothing like a kroj. Just wear my red taffeta. It'll coordinate with your red nails and your sweater. It's one night of the year, so it wouldn't hurt you to look . . ." Her mom rolled her eyes.

"Like what?" Lina's tone was more defensive than she intended.

"Normal—not like a fairy waltzing into the party."

"Better than pretending to be royalty." Lina waved slowly, her fingers flush against each other. The Tureks' annual black-tie affair was as grand as a wedding. Lina had grown tired of the formality and same scheduled activities. Nothing changed with the Tureks.

"It's called elegance." Her mom raised her head.

"I'm getting evergreen nails to match." Lina jutted her chin.

Her mom placed her hands on her hips. "Lina Maria Dvorak, this isn't a sorority event. You can wear that skirt with green nails when you're out with your friends."

Nothing changes with her, either. Lina took a deep breath. "I'd like to spend the holiday season wearing an ugly Christmas sweater—or in my case, the skirt—and drinking hot chocolate, not sipping overpriced wine. If God intended us to celebrate Christmas attending all these soirees, Jesus would've been born in a palace."

"Has Rich seen the skirt?" Her mother tossed a pound of margarine into a ceramic mixing bowl with such force it landed with a thud.

There she goes again, deferring to Rich. Is he my boyfriend or hers? Her family and the Tureks were like a medieval clan, living in the same neighborhood, attending the same church, even vacationing together. So, in her mom's eyes, the Tureks' son Rich hung the moon, especially once he joined her family's garden center and nursery.

After Rich and Lina broke up when they went off to separate universities, Lina's mom told her (and everyone else), "You will still marry Rich. You're meant for each other. You'll see."

Were her mom's words prophetic or just wishful thinking? Either way, Lina didn't expect to fall for Rich after she moved back to Traverse City to help launch a second location for Peonies and Pines. She couldn't resist his confidence as he garnered investors, found an ideal property, and created a duplicable model for future expansions. His business acumen enhanced his physical features—his cerulean blue eyes, sandy blond hair, and square jawline that initially drew her to him as a teen. "Did you hear me?" her mom asked.

Lina looked at her. "He'll be fine with it."

Her mom stopped mixing the dough. "You need to show him today. He deserves that."

"Why?" Lina scowled. *Deserves* was a strong word for referring to party attire.

"You're his date. Isn't that a good enough reason?"

Lina's phone rang. It was Rich.

Her mother glanced at Lina's phone as if nothing was private between them. "Are you going to answer him?"

"We're baking." Lina didn't want to take the call in case Mom was right about him disapproving the skirt.

"The yeast has to rise, anyway. You have time." Her mom's "Please" said she was tortured to let the call go.

"Fine," Lina hissed. She dashed to the back of the house as she took the call.

"Babe, are you at your mom's?" Rich asked. "I was concerned because you haven't answered my texts."

She stood in the unheated sunroom, shivering and soberly alert. "Sorry, I was in a hurry this morning. But I'm here. What's up?"

"Since things have been hectic—you know, with the expansion and the holidays and all." Rich cleared his throat. "We need to spend more quality time together." He paused. *Was he reading a script?* "I was thinking, we should hang out before the party. It's always a huge gathering, so it'll be difficult to have 'us' time."

His obvious unease caught her off guard. It was rare to hear him not in command of himself. "What's up, babe? We are always together at work and most evenings."

"That's why I'm emphasizing quality time. We talk too much about work, so how about we leave all that at the office and just hang out? I'll pick you up at five tomorrow."

Lina's throat constricted as her covert plans for tomorrow night neared the chopping block. "I promised Grands I'd pick her up around six thirty for the party."

"Love, Joey can pick up Grands."

Whoosh! The wind slammed sleets of snow on the windows. Lina stepped away from the panes as if they'd collapse in on her. "What's a few hours before the party when we have all day Sunday?"

"Because I need it for us. Isn't that a good enough reason?"

Great. He had tomorrow night planned but wanted to surprise her, to act "spontaneous." Like her mom, Rich was rigidly scheduled. He'd probably mapped out their next twenty to thirty years together. What was he planning now? Was her mom in on it? Lina didn't want to back down, but he'd pound like a battering ram until he'd break her defenses.

"Fine," she whispered. She'd find a way to leave the party without him.

After she hung up, she returned to the kitchen. "Rich will keep you grounded," her mother said, pouring flour into a large metal mixing bowl.

Suddenly, as if deciphering code, Lina understood the plan. *He's going to propose! That's why Mom insisted we get our nails done the afternoon of the party and is adamant I look regal.*

Lina looked at the oak floors—lightly polished, not a piece of dust or dirt visible. That was how everyone in their family would expect their marriage to be. "That's what you want," she murmured.

"What did you say?" her mother said with a raised tone.

"Nothing." Lina sighed, drained of mental energy after talking to Rich.

They spent the rest of the morning making eighty doughballs the size of walnuts. When their discussion turned to the nursery expansion, her mom's willingness to hear Lina's innovative ideas gave Lina a pinch of hope for their relationship.

Once they finished forming doughballs, Lina gave her mom a peck on the cheek. Then she took the doughballs to the condo she shared with Joey, hoping her twin brother's protein shakes would leave room for storing the dough overnight in their fridge.

December 17—Rohlicky Day 2

THE NEXT MORNING, THE flurries stopped, and the sky was blue gray with slight cloud cover. Lina picked up Grands at her senior living apartment and brought her to the condo. Although its kitchen was less spacious than her mom's, Lina preferred the warmth of her own home.

The fragrances of evergreen from the live Douglas fir in the living room and cranberry-orange from the diffuser in the kitchen aroused the sentiment of a joyful Christmas. Lina mixed egg whites in a copper bowl, while Grands, donning a new apron embroidered with bright red and green ornaments, used a small rolling pin to roll out chilled doughballs into circles.

A contemporary jazz rendition of "Christmas Time Is Here" piped through the TV in the living room and drifted into the open kitchen. Lina softly sang to the lyrics as the artist's ethereal voice mixed well with the song's smooth piano and crooning sax.

Lina and Grands worked in silence as they tapped their feet and swayed to the beat. When the music became too quiet to hear the lyrics, Lina looked toward the living room.

"Why did you turn that down?" she asked Joey, who stood pointing the remote at the TV.

"I can't hear myself think, much less talk." He walked into the kitchen and gave Grands a hug. "I'll pick you up at six thirty."

"Sorry, Grands, I forgot to tell you." Lina finished whipping. The egg whites were perfectly stiff. "Rich wants to meet me before the party."

"Oh, that's right." Grands frowned.

Hmm. Does Grands know Rich is proposing? Grands once told Lina that although Rich was a decent young man, he seemed too stiff for her flittering canary granddaughter.

Joey grabbed a blueberry muffin from the counter and walked toward the kitchen table.

Uh-oh! After she got home from her parents' house yesterday, she was too tired to notice she left the flyer on the table. Not wanting him to see it, she lunged to intercept him but was too late.

"What's this?" He grabbed the flyer and pointed to the name Bard Rhys she'd circled in yellow highlighter. When she saw the flyer at Third Coast Bakery early yesterday, her mouth gaped. Why was her ex performing here? Hadn't he looked down on the smaller market Traverse City provided musicians?

Even though they hadn't talked to or seen each other since April, she had to check him out now. Otherwise she couldn't get his name, his songs, and his well-being out of her mind. She'd find some way to sneak out of the Tureks' party to attend the folk concert. She could change into her green skirt, since it'd fit in perfectly with the concert's boho crowd and Bard. How many times did they wear matching ugly sweaters to Christmas parties?

"Have you mentioned this to Rich?" Joey's brows arched toward a lecture.

"I'm not married," Lina said with a sharpness meant to warn Joey to mind his own business. Normally, they got along unless his loyalty to Rich or their parents interfered with her freedom.

"I'd like to see Bard," Grands said in a singsong tone. "He's such a kindhearted young man."

Back when Lina had brought Bard home to meet the family, Grands accepted him, an outsider. Now, her time with Bard felt like a lifetime ago.

"You can't go tonight, anyway." Joey set down the flyer.

"I'm tired of everyone telling me what I can't do." Lina slammed her hand on the table so hard that a wooden sheep in the Nativity there fell on its side.

"Chill, sis. I'm looking out for you. Bard's a good guy, but he's not like us." Joey tapped his chest with his fist.

Lina rolled her eyes. "We Czechs aren't a different species of human."

Joey stood, wrapping his uneaten muffin in a napkin. "I'm off to the nursery. I know you'll do the right thing."

"I always do, even if it's not what everyone expects."

"Always have to distinguish yourself, don't you?" Joey crossed his arms.

"What's so wr—?" Seeing Grands shake her head, Lina heeded the wordless advice to take the gracious road.

Once Joey left, Lina approached Grands. "Rich is proposing tonight, isn't he?"

"Yes." Her grandmother's wince conveyed guilt for letting the cat out of the bag.

She shouldn't have cornered Grands, but Lina wanted a confirmation. Through the years, Lina confided in Grands about most things, especially about love and family.

"I want to still be Bard's friend. Is that wrong?" Lina's stomach churned.

"Not unless you say *yes* to Rich, dear."

"But Bard's not moving here, anyway." Was it possible he came up north more for her than for the concert?

"You should talk to him. What if he's reconsidered?" Grands raised her brows, something she did when advising Lina over a difficult decision.

"No, he was clear when he broke up." Lina swallowed, the words *broke up* stuck in her throat. She hadn't received closure from the abrupt end of their relationship eight months ago, when she announced she was moving back to Traverse City. That started a tug of war, him expecting her to move to his hometown of Ann Arbor, her insisting he could play music anywhere. As she explained about TC's music scene, he waved his hand and cut her off coldly midsentence. "I'm done." Then he stormed out of his living room.

How dare he cut her short and then walk off. He might as well have duct-taped her mouth shut. Leaving his apartment, Lina slammed his front door. Even though he called her a couple of hours later, she didn't answer or listen to his voice mail but blocked his number.

All her life, her mom refused to engage in debate but would change the subject, cutting Lina off midsentence or warning Lina would face discipline if she continued to argue. As a teen, Lina was grounded so much she spent more weekends at home than with her friends.

"Don't assume anything. We all can change, especially when it comes to love." The gentle words from Grand's brought Lina back to the kitchen.

"Maybe." Tapping the counter helped Lina think. "I suppose I should give him a chance to explain."

"Have you talked to him lately?" Grands asked.

"I will." Lina grabbed her phone and released his number from no-man's-land with one swift motion.

Dings shrilled, announcing voice-mail notifications. Bard had left ten messages from April to May. The first reacquainted her to his tenor voice with that slight raspy tone. "I don't know why you broke up and left. I want to work this out." The next queries filled her with regret. "Can't we work this out?" "Why aren't you calling me?" "Did you block me? You moved on that quick?"

The last message from May ushered in shame as his gracious sensibility reached out to her. "Whatever you decide, I want you to know I don't regret the past four years together. I still can't wrap my mind around this breakup, but I won't call you anymore. I still love and miss you."

She cried. Not hard, but long enough to purge the pain she'd locked up. She hadn't stopped loving him, but things were too complicated now. Grands touched Lina's back, her warm hand like a balm.

Once Lina caught her breath, she listened to the message Bard left yesterday. It was like he walked into her kitchen, hazel eyes gazing into hers, caramel hair casually brushing his shoulders. As his memory approached her with his slow, rhythmic gait, every step was a folk song, patient and relaxed.

Wanting him near, she listened to it again, putting it on speaker. "Hey, it's Bard. I called to say hi and see how you're doing. I'm in TC, going to perform at the City Opera House. I promised I wouldn't contact you, but since I'm this close, I wanted to see if you'd be up for coffee." She held her breath through his short pause. "And to tell you how sorry I am. I expected you to follow my career in Ann Arbor, but I realize I want you more. We can make this work if you're still interested. Please call."

Her anger toward him dissolved like yeast in warm water.

Desperate for a nugget of wisdom or insight, Lina glanced at Grands. "How did you know Grandpa was the one?"

"He could cut a rug." Grands hummed a soft tune of days gone by.

Lina smiled, then touched Grands on her arm. "Seriously."

Grands stopped rolling. "He never caged me."

Lina turned away. Rich loved her, but he didn't seem to appreciate her sanguine tendencies. How many times did he complain about her tardiness or ask her to tame her hyperboles? They shared insider jokes, though, and pulled the best pranks on Joey. They understood each other and their families and didn't need to explain their traditions or values.

But Bard let her be herself, accepting her spontaneity and adventurous nature. He'd been willing to drive wherever the road led them on a free Saturday. And they'd talked about how they'd merge his Welsh and her Czech traditions and even form new ones. Lina wondered if she (and perhaps Grands) was partially drawn to Bard because of his similarity to her Welsh Grandpa.

"You do what's best for you," Grands said.

"Rich is the ideal match. Organized, steady, and Czech." Lina nodded to convince herself more than Grands.

"Sounds like your mom talking."

"I don't know."

"Through the years, your mom and I butted heads on many things, but I realized part of it was my fault. I was afraid she wouldn't enjoy life if she remained so scheduled and rigid. But the harder I tried to make her like me, the more she rebelled. Babi told me that our differences were a gift from God."

"Humph!" Lina put her hands on her hips. "Why can't she learn your lesson?"

"She's still a work in progress, dear." Grands paused. "As we get older, the child becomes the parent. If you learn to understand her now, you'll have patience when she depends on you later."

"I'm trying." Lina bit her lip. She couldn't imagine her mom old and frail, much less relying on Lina.

"That's all you can do. Let God give you his strength."

Lina nodded as her thoughts cleared. "I want to see Bard."

"Call him, then."

"This decision affects us all. And maybe the nursery."

"You and Joey can lead the expansion." Grands straightened her posture.

"You think Rich would quit?" Lina's eyes grew wide.

"He's proud."

Lina couldn't respond as implications swam in her mind. To keep them at bay, she focused on finishing the rohlicky. She added the ingredients for the nut filling into the bowl and mixed them thoroughly. Then they put the filling—which Grands called the "meat"—into the middle of the dough circle. Grands applied her expertise, using her fingers to slowly roll the dough, seal the edges, and then curve it into a half-moon. Lina helped roll as they repeated the delicate process one by one until they had eighty pastries on baking sheets.

Grands gave Lina a kiss on her forehead. "Your choice is up to you."

After washing her hands, Lina turned off the music to hear herself think and then sat at the kitchen table, waiting for the timer to sound. She stared at the French doors that opened to the patio. The snow drifts, a few feet high from yesterday's flurries, seemed to want to come inside.

Grands sat next to Lina for a few minutes, holding her hand in silence until the timer went off. Lina hated to get up and break the tender moment. As she did, Grands walked into the living room and laid in the recliner.

While Lina remained in the kitchen, minding the rohlicky, Grands shared anecdotes of the many Christmases she had with Grandpa, combining their holiday traditions. Grandpa introduced an Advent calendar, and they filled it with chocolates for the kids. He always lit the Advent wreath each Sunday in December, hung mistletoe, and went caroling. Grands set Nativity scenes at each table, and they opened one gift on Christmas Eve. All the memories blew softly like the light snow outside. How many Christmas breaks did Lina spend at their house, curled between Grandpa and Grands in front of the fireplace?

By one o'clock that afternoon, the finished rohlicky cooled on the counter. Walking past the kitchen table to fetch her keys, Lina noticed that the sheep earlier toppled in the Nativity now stood near the manger, longingly gazing at Baby Jesus. Lina smiled at Grands' gesture.

After Lina dropped Grands off, she made it to the nail salon ten minutes early. Her mom thanked her for being ahead of time and rewarded Lina with a broad smile.

By three thirty, Lina was home, sitting in her bedroom. Wanting to rest her eyes, she played Proverbs 1 on audio, listening for an answer to her dilemma. Even a whisper would help. She wanted to honor her parents, especially her mother, but did that mean she had to marry Rich?

When God seemed silent, she opened her eyes and looked outside, watching the snow waltz slowly down to the ground.

By four, she got ready and slipped into her mother's long red taffeta skirt. It touched the floor and was heavy, swishing as she walked. She put on her three-inch heels so the skirt came to her ankles. She groaned as the mirror reflected the image of a middle-aged socialite—not the look she wanted to convey on her engagement. *Oh well, I'm honoring Mom with my outfit, but at least I have Douglas-fir nails.*

When she fixed her blond hair in a chignon, she needed something more, so she put sprigs of ivy around the bun. Now she looked more like herself.

She grabbed her phone, pulled up the right contact, and pressed Send.

"Hi," she said.

"Hello." Rich's voice was defensive enough to hold down a fortress.

"I've decided what I want." Lina's tone was confident.

"About tonight? Bard?"

Lina's back became stiff as she realized he'd heard the news. "Joey told you, didn't he?"

"I expected you to tell me earlier."

Hearing Rich's hurt tone, she wondered if he felt disrespected by her omission. "I'm sorry I didn't. I was afraid you'd object, but I should've been forthright. That's why I'm calling. How about we excuse ourselves from the party around eight or nine? We could go listen to folk music. Or if you don't want to hear Bard, we could look at Christmas lights. Or just sit at a coffee shop, spending quality time together."

"We're not listening to Bard. And you know it's our party tradition to eat dessert at eight. Dad gives the annual Christmas toast right after, and then we listen to a musician perform Christmas classics. We never leave before ten."

"Fine, but let's promise to make some of our own traditions. To pick something unique each year, so we keep our plans fresh and fun.

Maybe we could go on a cruise for Christmas sometime." Lina talked quickly as her heart raced with possibilities.

"No, Christmas is shored up by rituals. It's how it's always done. Look, I've got to finish getting ready, and then I'll pick you up."

"Don't come." Lina gripped her chest, preparing for his reaction.

"Unbelievable! You still care for that outsider?"

"I care about you, but we're not right for each other." She stared at the multicolored lights shining from the Charlie Brown–sized Christmas tree in her room. "Sorry, I can't marry you."

"We'll see how you feel tomorrow." His tone, elevated with sarcasm, was tinged with enough of his rigidity to solidify what her future with him would be like.

She hung up, then texted Bard. "I'll be there by nine."

Story Inspiration

My paternal grandmother's parents emigrated to the United States from Czechoslovakia in the early 1900s. Like Lina and Grands in this story, my grandma always moved to her own beat. So, it wasn't surprising that although she was engaged to a Czech American (her three siblings married Czech or Slovak Americans), she fell in love with and married my grandpa, a Welsh and German American.

In their honor, I'm donating my anthology proceeds to International Community Outreach in Tulsa, Oklahoma (icotulsa.org) serving international students and refugees in Oklahoma and the Czech Republic.

About Sarah

WHAT'S LOVE GOT TO do with it? Everything! Sarah Soon's background—first as a young girl adopted into a loving Christian family and then as an adult not marrying until her forties (yes, you read that right)—has given her rich material to explore the dynamics of love and relationships. Her stories center on imperfect protagonists needing to experience God's transformative power so they can find love, sustain healthier relationships, and experience healing.

When Sarah isn't writing, she's asking her husband for his feedback (he's a story nerd too!), enjoying nature (especially hiking or kayaking), and fellowshipping with family, friends, and her church community. She also enjoys traveling and learning about different cultures.

Sarah loves interacting with readers, especially through her monthly newsletters, where subscribers offer feedback as beta readers and vote on significant elements of her book journey, including book covers, story titles, and character names. She believes it takes a village to publish a novel.

Join Sarah's community by signing up for her monthly newsletter at sarahsoon.com.

35

Benediction

by Linda Sammaritan

SHARONA USED THE BACK OF her gloved hand to scratch the itch on the tip of her nose. After three years of shelving stock at a big-box store, she'd never adjusted to the dust and whatever other grime came with cardboard and strapping tape. Itch relieved, she continued the transfer of balsam-scented candles to an eye-level shelf.

She glanced down as a second, unopened carton slid across the floor to join the half-empty one beside her.

"You got room for one more, or you want me to take this one back?" Birdie's sunshine-yellow tennis shoe toed the box a little closer to its twin.

"I've got enough space."

"Good." Birdie closed her eyes and inhaled deeply. "I can smell almost-real Christmas trees even through the plastic."

One more allergy for Sharona. The fake scents messed with her vocal cords almost as much as the boxes did, and both were no help for recovering from throat surgery.

Birdie breathed in again, then opened her eyes. "And look how beautiful it all is!" She spun in a circle, her arms wide as if embracing every garland, every string of lights, and every roll of Christmas wrap. She cocked her head to one side, reminding Sharona of a sparrow responding to other birds' songs. "You can even *hear* Christmas."

Sharona listened to the incessant music piped throughout the store, her accompaniment for eight hours a day. At the moment, upbeat voices were singing the lyrics to "Santa Claus Is Comin' to Town."

Yeah, she'd done enough crying and pouting to jinx her chances at happy surprises from Santa Claus. *Or* God. Maybe she didn't deserve happy surprises.

"So what do you think?" Birdie hadn't stopped talking. She hardly ever did.

"Of Christmas music?"

The sparkle in Birdie's eyes flickered for a moment, then burned bright. "The Christmas concert at my church. A college choir is coming in, and it's free. I thought you might like to go since you had a whole career teaching music to kids. You told me you used to sing in a college choir, right?"

Two hours or more with Birdie sounded exhausting. How much cheer and chatter could a person take? Still, Birdie was the only person Sharona could describe as a friend these days. The short bundle of energy was probably twenty years her senior and never seemed to resent the wall Sharona purposely put up between herself and anyone else.

"Which choir?"

"Wellspring University. It's about an hour past the state line."

Wellspring. That complicated her decision. It was hard enough to listen to vocal music at all when she could no longer sing properly, but could she sit through a concert watching a new generation from her alma mater? Would they sing any of the pieces used thirty years ago? Did they still finish with "The Benediction"? Could she handle long-gone happy memories?

Birdie's bright, expectant smile waited for an answer.

Better not pout. "Okay. When is it?"

"Tomorrow night. Seven o'clock." Birdie nearly twittered with joy. "You know where Grace Baptist is?"

"Yes."

"I'll meet you inside the front door. Maybe fifteen minutes ahead? The place fills up quick. We're not that big of a church, you know."

"Okay. Six forty-five then." Sharona looked at the cartons of work ahead of her.

"I'll drop around and see how you're doing in about an hour." Birdie pivoted the dolly she'd just emptied and rolled it down the aisle. "What should I bring over to you?"

"Meet me in aisle ten with the angel tree-toppers."

"Got it." Birdie rolled the empty dolly ahead of her with an off-key "Sing choirs of angels" spouting from her lips.

SHARONA ALWAYS LOOKED FORWARD to Thursday nights. Ever since Garrett graduated from college and returned to Richmond for a graduate degree in business, he claimed he loved the opportunity for a homecooked meal once a week. She had the feeling their mom-and-son dinners were an excuse for Garrett to check on her. Sure, she'd been a basket case three years ago, complete with antianxiety meds, but she'd gotten much better.

Garrett blew in through the kitchen door along with a blast of frigid air. Gone were the days of a heated, attached, three-car garage. Sharona's portion of the house settlement afforded her this cozy little rental offering nothing more luxurious than a carport. At least it kept her old Toyota from being buried in snow.

"Man, it got cold today. What's for dinner?" Garrett sniffed the air.

"I've had stew simmering in the crockpot all day. It should melt in your mouth and warm your insides all at the same time."

He tossed his coat over a spare chair and sat at his usual place. "And to think I used to hate that stuff when I was a kid."

She brought bowls full of tomatoes and beef to the table one at a time, steaming and fragrant with spices. A crusty loaf of bread already rested between the two place settings. "So, any progress on applying for internships?"

He allowed the spoonful of broth to touch his lips, then hastily dropped it into the bowl and buttered a slice of bread instead.

"I'm still looking for a position at a little start-up corporation, so I'll be ready to start my own in a couple of years." He grinned. "Then I'll hire you for the front office."

What a shame that he felt the need to support his "helpless" forty-nine-year-old mother. Worse, she was tempted to allow such a thing to happen. To depend on your own child like that? It wasn't fair to him.

Sharona blew on her spoon filled with stew. "Where have you looked so far?"

"Places like phone stores and restaurants." He laughed when he caught her eye. "I know—I don't cook. Anyway, I'll aim for one of those if I can't find what I want. At least they have blueprints to follow if I want to buy into a franchise."

"You'll figure it out."

"Dad already offered me an internship with his company. But that's a huge corporation. The only way I'll take it is if everyone else turns me down."

When Garrett started a neighborhood lawnmowing business at the age of eleven, his father had labeled him "a natural entrepreneur." But by the time Garrett was sixteen and talking about owning a karate school, John hadn't been so enthusiastic. "You'll never get rich doing that," he'd said.

Sharona allowed herself a small inward smile. Her son couldn't be bought off.

AFTER GARRETT'S DEPARTURE, Sharona stacked plates and bowls in the dishwasher. The phone chirped. Elena.

"Is Garrett still there?" Elena never bothered with "hello."

"He left about ten minutes ago.

She wouldn't join them for dinner but always wanted to know the latest after her brother left. Sharona clicked the phone to speaker and continued putting the kitchen to rights.

"Did you talk about what he wanted for Christmas?"

"No, we didn't discuss it."

"It would've been helpful to know what he might like." Elena's irritation vibrated through the phone.

"Get him something he can eat. A food basket. A gift card to a restaurant. He's always hungry."

"Seems kind of impersonal." Elena's voice brightened. "Daddy called today. He's got four tickets for the yuletide concert. Really good seats, too."

Of course. John could easily drop a thousand dollars on four tickets. "That's a perfect gift for you, honey. Enjoy the evening."

"There's a teensy problem, though."

"Oh?"

"Yeah. The tickets are for Christmas Eve."

He. Did. Not.

"I see."

Christmas Eve was scheduled to be Sharona's time with Elena and Garrett this year. She could hear John's arguments already. *You'll have the kids all day. I'll just start Christmas a little early with them.* And John would insist on keeping his entire Christmas Day as well. No wonder she always felt emotionally exhausted.

But her boy wouldn't break the original agreement. Garrett would stick with her on Christmas Eve.

"So, no ideas for my baby brother?" Elena was happy to return to her original subject after dropping the dirty bomb of bad news.

"If you want to know his wish list, why don't you ask him yourself?"

"That would be too obvious."

As if Elena knew how to be subtle.

Elena switched channels. "Well, what do you think I should get for Daddy?"

Struck dumb, Sharona glared at the phone. Her daughter was twenty-five years old, totally independent, and for some reason couldn't acknowledge that her "perfect" daddy had fractured the family. "I suggest you ask his wife." She gently clicked the red phone icon.

There. Momentary satisfaction.

BIRDIE SHOWED UP IN THE break room while Sharona was still stowing her gear in a locker.

"Ready for tonight? I'm so excited. George and I are taking a couple of tenors home with us. They board with the congregation, you know—spend the tour visiting people in their homes after each concert. I can't wait to find out where they're from originally."

Sharona wasn't sure she could muster the energy for Birdie and a concert. Since the previous night, she'd been trying again to figure out where she'd gone wrong in the mothering department. All she wanted tonight was a glass of wine and old reruns of *The Andy Griffith Show*. Adulterous affairs never appeared in that show's plot, and Sharona could whisper-croak along with Andy's crooner voice, nobody around to listen.

"Since George is going with you, I hope you won't mind if I don't attend after all."

"Not attend?" The light in Birdie's eyes blinked out.

Sharona hunched her shoulders against the expected onslaught of disappointed words. "Last night was rough."

Concert seemingly forgotten, Birdie patted Sharona's cheek. "Elena or John?"

"Just thinking about Christmas Day without family. And maybe how I deserve it. Maybe Elena's right. With my botched surgery and depression, John was driven into the arms of someone easier to live with."

Birdie's tender smile tightened. "That man was waiting for an excuse to leave for years, and the whole town knew it, even if you didn't." Her finger pecked at Sharona's shoulder. "Deep down, I think you *did* know it. You just believed marriage was for a lifetime, so you put up with him."

Sharona stepped back and stood straight. "So you think I should've been the one to leave?"

"I didn't say that." Birdie peered up at her. "I said you stuck up for what you believed in." She glanced around the near-empty break room, a little late if checking for eavesdropping ears. "Marriage isn't rainbows and unicorns, not even with me and my George, and he's a saint. But you got handed compost and cow manure and still managed to raise good kids and inspire your students." She nodded. "I went to many of your elementary school concerts to watch my grandkids, you know."

No, Sharona didn't know. Not about Birdie's presence at winter and spring concerts and, at the time, not about John's reputation around town. Life had been too busy inside her cocoon of classes and performances, where she'd only stepped away to run Elena to jazz dance or Garrett to karate or to slap food on the table for whoever was home on a given night.

Birdie rubbed Sharona's shoulder, as if trying to ease the pain where her finger had jabbed a minute earlier. "Now that we've established you were a great mother and excellent teacher, let's also talk truth about this concert." She didn't allow time for any objection. "You want to hear that music more than I do. I'll bet you even sang the same kind of music in your college days. And you deserve to do something kind for yourself. You deserve to hear that music. Am I right?"

Sharona couldn't manage a response. *Was* Birdie right?

"Of course, I'm right. Here." Birdie rummaged in the pocket of her work apron and pulled out a sheet of folded paper. "This is the program. All the hosts for the choir members got one. See if you recognize any of the songs." She shoved the paper against Sharona's chest.

Sharona plucked the paper from Birdie's fist, holding it between thumb and index finger as if it might burst into flame. Unfolding it, she scanned the list of selections. Fourth one down, the "Magnum Mysterium." And the final piece, "The Benediction." The choir continued the tradition. Longing to hear the harmonies and lyrics one more time, she returned the program to Birdie and nodded.

"I'll be there."

But would she be able to bear it?

IN A BITING WIND, Sharona scurried up the steps toward the open front door of Grace Baptist Church. As soon as she slipped inside, she spotted Birdie's scarlet coat amid the blacks and grays filling the foyer.

Sharona tapped her friend's shoulder, and Birdie turned away from the slight, elderly gentleman at her side. "You got here! Lovely!"

Was she surprised? Sharona always kept her word.

"I already placed my purse on one of the middle pews along with two programs, so we have our seats." She turned back to the man. "George, this is Sharona. You've heard me talk about her." She winked at Sharona. "And you hear me talk about George all the time."

George extended his hand, but before they could shake, Birdie grabbed both their arms. "Let's hustle, now. People will respect where I've saved our places for only so long."

She chattered on down the center aisle as George gave Sharona a lopsided smile. On finding the correct row, Birdie directed Sharona to enter first, then she followed, with George last in line. He helped his wife shrug off her coat and laid it neatly over the back of the pew, smoothing it down before inviting Birdie to sit. That minuscule act of tenderness nearly undid Sharona. And the music hadn't even started yet.

Lights blinked on and off, signaling the crowd to take their seats. A few acquaintances from her teaching days nodded to Sharona as they passed by her row. The robed choir filed in, about forty members strong, and the pastor, dressed casually in sweater and slacks, led the congregation in prayer before welcoming the choir director.

The lights went dark except for those above the choir. The director lifted her baton. Every choir member focused on it. How well Sharona remembered. Her heartbeat accelerated with anticipation of the first notes.

A quiet, pure *alleluia* began with the sopranos. Fifteen voices blended into one. The tenors added a counter melody, followed by the altos. Then the basses contributed robust depths of praise. For the first time in years, Sharona yielded to the bliss of harmonies.

Uncharacteristically silent, Birdie left her seat for a stretch at intermission. Her quiet return allowed Sharona to bask in the beauty of the preceding hour. Again the sanctuary darkened, and she sank into the Baroque polyphony of Bach, Bender's modern and beautiful dissonances, and African djembe drums accompanying an otherwise a cappella choir. Finally, it was time for "The Benediction."

Exactly as Sharona had done years ago, the choir left the stage risers, each member picking up a small candle from a box on the front pew as they all encircled the entire congregation. The director floated to the middle of the church in the center aisle.

The pastor, front and center, stood behind a table holding a tall candle. As soon as he lit the taper, the lights above the risers dimmed, then went out. Only one flame pushed back the darkness in the church. Two choir members on either side of the table leaned their candles into the single flame, creating three. Two little candles lit two more, again and again, until a ring of fire surrounded the audience. All was ready.

The baton lifted. Dipped.

"The Lord bless thee, and keep thee." The full choir's restrained pianissimo wafted through Sharona's entire being.

"The Lord make his face shine upon thee, and be gracious unto thee." Gentle notes and rhythms swirled around her.

Sharona yearned to feel God's face shine on her again. She watched one choir figure standing three rows forward from her own. Coils of long, dark hair rested on her robe. Her face reflected the purity and naive beauty Sharona once possessed.

The girl's lips seemed to follow the soprano line. "The Lord lift up his countenance upon thee." She smiled as she sang. Angelic. Sharona couldn't look away.

"And give thee peace."

Sharona whispered the words of the last line. Was God willing to bless Sharona with peace?

"And give thee peace."

Silence. The director would decide when to break it.

The soprano looked directly at Sharona. How could that be? The candle in the girl's hand should blind her to faces in the audience.

Sharona's peripheral vision caught the slight rise of the baton.

"Amen." The choir sang through the last consonant, the benediction drifting into a hum of "nnnnnnnnnnn" as the chords shifted to the final resolution.

Sharona remained transfixed by the soprano's beatific smile. As the amen faded away, the girl nodded to her, and amazing peace descended.

Birdie's hand slipped into Sharona's and squeezed. Sharona returned the pressure.

As one, the choir whispered a puff of air and snuffed out their candles. They walked toward the front, silent, both lines meeting in the center and exiting in the same direction from which they had entered.

The single flame on the table remained, and cold ashes in Sharona's heart stirred with renewed warmth.

Story Inspiration

MANY YEARS AGO, I WAS a choir soprano whose attention was drawn to a middle-aged lady in the audience. She was beautiful and looked weary, and as we sang "The Benediction," her eyes remained riveted on me. The song died away, and I smiled at her, sensing God wanted me to demonstrate his love for her. Her brows rose in surprise, and she didn't return the smile, but she continued to watch me as I turned to exit down the side aisle of the church. I hope I was a blessing.

I'm donating my proceeds from this anthology to Thirsty Ground International (thirstyground.org), an organization conducting disaster relief and development projects around the world.

About Linda

Linda Sammaritan writes realistic fiction, mostly for kids ages ten to fourteen. She has completed a middle-grade trilogy, World Without Sound, based on her own experiences growing up with a deaf sister. Book 1, *Reaching into Silence*, was a semifinalist in the American Christian Fiction Writers Carol Awards and the ACFW Genesis Contest and a finalist in the ACFW First Impressions Contest.

Linda always figured she'd teach teens and tweens until school authorities presented her with a retirement wheelchair and rolled her out the door. God changed those plans when he gave her a growing passion for writing fiction. In May 2016, she blew goodbye kisses to her students and dedicated her work hours to becoming an author.

A wife, mother of three, and grandmother to eight, Linda regales her youngest grandchildren with "Nona stories," tales of her childhood. Maybe one day those stories will be in picture books!

Visit lindasammaritan.com to learn more about Linda and her writing.

A Touch of Fudge and Romance

by Mari Eygabroad

JACKIE HELD HER BREATH as she read the email from the mission committee. She thought she would be going overseas to teach right after graduation six months ago. After seven applications, she was beginning to see that missionary teacher positions were filling quicker than she could even get in her applications. She reread the email three times to be sure she understood. Yes! She was being offered a three-year teaching position at a missionary school in Zimbabwe!

But what about Michal? The perfect guy she'd been dating for almost a year had been working hard to get in his flight hours, but actually how close was he to finishing and going on the mission field? She calculated in her head that he might have at least one more year before finishing school. The application process to any organization is about three months, followed by at least a year of raising support.

Where is our relationship going? Would he be open to a long-distance relationship? Will he wait for me?

She closed her laptop and sent him a text. *Can we talk?*

Her phone rang about a minute later. "Hey, babe! I'm just getting dressed for the party. What's up?" Michal sounded very cheerful. Getting ready for the Christmas party must be filling him with holiday spirit.

"Mick, I got it." She paused. "I got an email from the mission committee today. They offered me the Zim position—a three-year contract."

The phone was quiet.

"Mick?"

"Yeah, I'm here." His voice cracked a little.

"Mick, you know I've been dreaming about this since I was a kid. I know three years is a long time to be apart. But you still have flight hours and application processes, and I—well . . ." She struggled for words.

"Have you accepted it?" Mick replied in a hurried tone.

"No, I haven't replied yet."

"Please don't do anything yet. Let's talk more after the party."

"Mick, I need to know where we, you and me, are going—"

"Jace, please. Can we talk after the party?"

Jackie took a deep breath and let it out slowly. "Yeah, okay. I'll see you there."

"I love you." Mick quickly added.

"Love you, too." She pressed the red disconnect button, stared at Mick's picture on her phone wallpaper, then hugged the phone to her chest. A tear rolled down her cheek.

She pulled herself together and started dressing for the party. She'd wear her hair down tonight. Michal once told her he liked the way her long brown curls flowed down her back and accentuated her big brown eyes. She donned her traditional Christmas sweater and opted for jeans and boots this year. Washington State wasn't known to get a ton of snow, but this year was an exception.

Arlington Community Church, where she'd attended since moving to Washington State from Africa twelve years ago, was expecting a large turnout for their annual Christmas party. All the students of the Mission Aviation Training Academy were invited as usual. Mingling with the aviation students, some of whom grew up overseas like her, gave Jackie a sense of belonging.

Some of the treat tables were already set up when she entered the church sanctuary. She took a piece of Michal's fudge from a plate and lifted it to her nose. As she breathed in the sweet aroma of chocolate, coffee, and peppermint, memories of Christmases past flooded her mind. Taking a bite, she closed her eyes and whispered to herself. "Mmmm. So good." She gently placed the rest of the fudge in her mouth and walked to the sound booth, where she stood on her tiptoes and asked the DJ to play Phil Wickham's Christmas album. Turning toward the dance floor, she saw Michal helping to set up the treat tables. She smiled and bit her lip.

Her godfather approached, carrying a box for one of the vendors. Seeing him reminded Jackie of her dad, who "Uncle" Stu served with in the airlines before becoming a consultant for mission aviation. He stopped next to her, nodded toward Michal, and spoke in his captain's voice. "He's a keeper, that one."

"I know," Jackie said with a smile as he continued walking. Remembering her earlier conversation with Michal made her smile fade a little. Could she keep her relationship with Michal and fulfill her dream of serving on the mission field?

When the music started, Michal glanced up and caught her watching him. He flashed his signature half smile and finished setting up the table he was working on. Then he walked across the sanctuary to join her by the sound booth.

"There you are," he said as he wrapped his arms around her. She melted like she had every time he'd touched her over the last year. Though they agreed not to kiss until they were engaged, she longed for the touch of his lips against hers.

Michal released his embrace, gently nudged her away from him while holding her arms, and held her gaze. She loved how the Christmas lights accentuated his bright green eyes. "First," he said as he put his hand on Jackie's cheek and ran his thumb across her bottom lip, "you've been stealing my fudge. You have a little bit on your lip."

Jackie felt a tingle down her spine, and her pulse quickened. She offered a sheepish grin and whispered a thank-you. A mere year ago, this man who drove her crazy with every touch wasn't part of her life. He wrapped his arms around her again, and her worries seemed to fade. Resting her head on his chest, she let her thoughts drift back to this time last year.

THE SANCTUARY WAS DECORATED for the yearly Christmas bash, featuring three trees on the stage, each with multicolored lights and ornaments. White icicle lights trailed along the crown molding in broad arcs. Tables draped with red, green, and gold cloths lined both sides of the room like a runway. The various items covering them included locally handmade gifts, books, and desserts—chocolates, cookies, pies, and other festive confections.

Jackie stood near the doorway by a table covered with chocolate treats, her long brown curls pulled up into a loose, messy bun. Her flashy Christmas sweater provided a dramatic contrast to the black pencil skirt that fit snuggly around her slim hips and modestly covered her knees. Black pumps with small gold bows completed her festive ensemble.

Uncle Stu approached with two cups of punch and gave her a little hip bump, his playful greeting since she had returned to America. He was tall and muscular, wore his hair in a military cut, and was usually poised. But tonight, he wore a gaudy blue Christmas suit covered in snowmen, gift boxes, and snowflakes. How he managed to be so proper and playful at the same time always baffled her. As the sounds of Phil Wickham's "Hark the Harold Angels Sing" filled the room, he handed her a cup. "I knew I'd find you here."

"Thanks." Jackie set the drink on the table and swayed to the music. "And just how did you know that?"

"Well, the best spot at any Christmas party is by the treats!" He placed a piece of fudge in his mouth.

"Too true! If I gain twenty pounds this Christmas, blame Gretchen. She left me alone with all these goodies!"

"Hey, speaking of— Why are you all alone? Weren't you supposed to come here with Alex? I thought you two were hitting it off?" He took a drink of punch.

"He's not really my type. Also, he said he wanted to pursue other options. I'm guessing that means he already has someone else in mind. I'm not sure he was up for the missionary life anyway." She eyed the plate of fudge she'd been picking away at. "It seems this fudge is the only thing I'll be holding this Christmas." She smooshed a piece between her thumb and finger, enjoying how it formed to them.

"I'm sorry, sweetheart. That's his loss. There's a lucky guy out there for you."

"I know. And I know I have a lot on my plate right now with graduating from college in June and hopefully going on the mission field—somewhere. But I also want to be married and have a family. I don't want to settle for just anyone, though." She put the fudge in her mouth, leaving a smear of chocolate on her fingers.

"God sees you. He'll send the perfect guy when the time is right." Uncle Stu wrapped one arm around her shoulders, then cleared his throat and nodded toward her fudge-covered hand. "But you may want to work on your table manners." He gave her a playful grin and handed her a Christmas-patterned napkin. "You wouldn't want to make a mess on that *fabulous* Christmas sweater."

Jackie laughed, stuck her tongue out, and pretended to smear chocolate over her face. "Hey, I love my Christmas sweater! It's sparkly." She set her fudge on a green plastic plate and pulled out the bottom hem of her sweater with her clean hand, admiring the glittering outlines of Christmas ornaments. "And *you* don't have any room to talk!" She gestured at his suit.

He laughed and looked down. "Touché."

She took the napkin and cleaned the chocolate off her hands. "Anyway, I just feel like guys I meet don't want deep connections."

"I understand. But some people do want closer relationships. They're just hard to find. That's why you cherish them when you find them.

"It just seems like it was easier to connect with my friends in Africa than with any of the people in my classes here. Take Alex, for example. He never wanted to talk about anything other than school or parties. When I was young, my friends and I would talk about how we saw God working in our lives. You know, stuff that matters." Jackie laughed. "I had one friend who used to push me down in the mud, but that was just kind of our thing."

"Are you still in touch with any of them?"

"No, I think my parents have kept in touch with some of their parents, but I'm not sure what any of them are up to now."

"You haven't connected well with anyone since you've been here?"

"I do have friends. But it's hard to even sit down for coffee for an hour to actually talk—everyone is so busy here." Jackie sighed. "I know it's probably not true, but in Africa, things just seemed slower and more about relationships. And I'm not just talking about guys. My girlfriends here keep it pretty shallow, too." She put her head on Uncle Stu's shoulder and adopted a mock whine. "Why is this so hard?" Phil Wickham's "Joy to the World" came over the speakers.

"Have you ever thought about going back?" Uncle Stu asked.

"To Africa?" Jackie looked at him with wide eyes.

"Yeah." He shrugged.

"I'd love to! I thought about going with Mom and Dad on their short-term trip, but I'm so close to finishing school. Plus, I'd rather go for a long term."

"Well, I'm sure the Lord is already making a way for you to go."

"Maybe. And I could go anywhere." Jackie placed the last corner of her fudge in her mouth and mindlessly grabbed another piece. "Uncle Stu, do you know who made this? It tastes a lot like Mom's."

"No, I don't. But your mom's fudge is pretty tasty!"

A young man about Jackie's age approached the table and gave a slight cough, politely interrupting their conversation. "Sorry, hi. Are you enjoying my fudge?" His accent was undoubtedly out of place in this Pacific Northwestern town.

Jackie looked up. With her mouth partly opened, she stared, captivated by his bright emerald eyes and dark, messy hair. It looked like he'd attempted a faux hawk hairstyle that didn't quite get there but looked even better somehow, neatly tapered, long on the top and short on the sides. Suddenly aware of her overindulgence, she handed her fudge to Uncle Stu and wiped her hands on her napkin again. "You made this? It's delicious!"

"Dankie—I mean, thank you." Jackie's ears perked up at the familiar "Thank you" in the Afrikaans language she grew up hearing. He reached out his hand. "I'm Michal."

"I'm Jackie." She shook his hand. "Nice to meet you, Mee-khal."

Michal looked surprised, then almost proud. "Truly a pleasure to meet you. Not many people can pronounce my name, yet you said it perfectly." He searched her eyes, almost as if seeking a lost treasure. He held her hand a little longer than expected, and her pulse quickened.

Uncle Stu cleared his throat.

Michal pulled his hand away and ran it through his dark hair, then rested it on the back of his head. Jackie took a deep breath, looked down, and ran her finger along the table. Uncle Stu extended his hand.

"Stu Sheffield. Nice to meet you."

Michal gave a firm handshake. "Pleasure to meet you, sir."

"Well-mannered," Uncle Stu said, turning to Jackie. "I like this guy."

Her eyes widened. "Uncle Stu!" she said through gritted teeth.

The music started playing a bit too loudly. Jackie was thankful for the distraction. They looked over at the DJ. He gave a little wave as if to say "I'll fix it" and adjusted the music to a suitable volume.

"Sho, anyway, I'm glad you like the fudge." Michal's voice cracked. "I hadn't made it in a while. My mum got the recipe from an American friend years ago. We used to make it together, and she gave me the recipe when I left."

"Oh. Where are you from? Wait, don't tell me." Jackie rested her elbow on her arm and tapped her temple, then called up her own South African accent. "Are you from . . . South Africa?"

"Whoa, nice." His "nice" sounded more like "noice." "Yeh, how did you know? Have you been?"

"Well, I grew up in Lesotho. Your accent sure takes me back to my childhood days."

"Serious? I grew up near there as well. In Ladybrand."

"Oh, yeah?" Jackie looked at Michal, trying to figure out what was so familiar about him. "Ladybrand, eh? We used to go there with our homeschool group once a week." She tilted her head a little. "Were you part of—" She stopped herself. "Nah, it couldn't be." She waved her hand and thought about the homeschool friends she had as a kid and her friend Mick. She could still see his soft green eyes and sandy blond hair.

He was only twelve when we left Lesotho for America. I wonder what he looks like now.

Phil Wickham's voice danced through the sanctuary. Jackie closed her eyes and started swaying and singing along with "Gloria in Excelsis Deo." She could always get lost in a worship song, Christmas or not.

"So, Michal . . ." Uncle Stu pronounced the name more like "Michael." "What brings you to the States?"

"Oh, I'm on a student visa, studying mission aviation at the academy."

Mission aviation? Jackie opened her eyes. She wanted to know more about this mysterious South African guy with delicious fudge, but she did not want to appear too eager after what had happened with Alex. She busied herself rearranging the treats on the table while listening to the two men chat.

"MATA? Really?" Uncle Stu said. "I have a friend who teaches there." He took a bite of fudge.

Huh, if Michal is studying at MATA, he'll probably be here for at least a year, maybe two.

"Is it?" Michal asked.

Jackie looked up and smirked at Uncle Stu's quizzical reaction to the Afrikaans phrase, thankful she was now not the only one speaking South Africanisms.

"What's his name?" Michal asked. "Might I have met him?"

Jackie butted in. "Probably not. It's my dad, Jake Harten. He's actually back in your neck of the woods these days."

"Jake Harten? Jake's your dad?" Michal looked at Jackie with wide eyes.

"Yep!" Jackie stood tall and smiled.

Michal stared at Jackie. "Wait. You're Jackie Harten?" He was silent for a moment. "Jace?" he exclaimed.

Jackie froze. *How does he know "Jace"?* No one called her that except family and— She stared at Michal. Her heart pounded. Millions of thoughts ran through her head. *Ladybrand. Homeschool. Michal. Mick?* She finally found her voice. "Mick?"

"Jace! It is you! My goodness!" Michal's voice raised and carried through the sanctuary, drawing attention from people shopping at the gift tables.

Her eyes glistened with tears. "Not possible. Is it really you?" She squeezed between the tables, knocking over her cup of punch. "Oh my gosh!"

She threw her arms around his waist and held on tight. Michal returned her embrace. His arms felt strong around her as his broad shoulders and well-over-six-foot frame practically swallowed her petite body. He smelled like her dad did when he came home from work, part dark chocolate body spray and part aviation gas.

"Oh my goodness, Mick! It's been ages!"

As Uncle Stu picked up the cup that had fallen over and cleaned up a spill of punch, he glanced up at them with a playful smile. "So, you two know each other?"

Jackie pulled away from their hug and looked at Uncle Stu. She wiped her tears with her sleeve. "Uncle Stu, this is Mick, one of my closest friends in South Africa." She turned back to Mick. "Not so much a boy anymore! I didn't even recognize you!"

"And you're not that li'l half-pint I used to push into the mud," Michal retorted.

"No. No, I'm not." Jackie smoothed her skirt and stood as tall as she could, then giggled.

"Oh, you're that friend." Uncle Stu smiled.

She cleared her throat and looked up at Michal. "Wow. What's it been? Ten—eleven years!" A strand of her dark brown hair came loose from her messy bun, and she tucked it behind her ear. "How are you? How long have you been here? What have you been up to?" She flushed over how her questions sprayed him like bullets from a Gatling gun.

Michal waded through the barrage. "Yeh, I'm good. My student visa was approved in July. I came in August to start school. Since the weather's been bad with the early snow, there's not been much flying. I went home last month to help Mum and have a short visit and just got back last week."

"Oh, I miss your mom. How is she?"

"She's good. Yeh. Actually, when she gave me that fudge recipe, she told me she got it from your mum."

"I knew it!" Jackie turned to Uncle Stu. "Didn't I say it tasted like Mom's?"

Uncle Stu nodded, grinning at them from ear to ear.

Jackie felt her face get hot. She turned to Michal and gave him a playful slug on the arm. "So, mission aviation, huh?"

Michal looked at his arm and chuckled. "Yeh! I always admired what your dad does. And being a pilot is just a cool job anyway." He half smiled at her, maybe trying to look cool.

She thought he looked more than cool. *Is this really happening?* "Yeah, it's okay, I guess." She winked.

He furrowed his brow. "So, what's your dad doing in South Africa?"

"He's working with Mission Aviation Fellowship. The Lesotho program is shorthanded, so he and mom are helping out. They'll probably be back sometime next year, but you never know with these things. I may join them after graduation. Who knows?" She sighed. "Oh, Mick, it's so good to see you!"

"It's good to be seen." Michal smirked. "And you look amazing." Phil Wickham's "This Year for Christmas" started playing. "Would you like to dance?"

Jackie chuckled and took the hand he offered. "Do you know this album?"

"Oh yeah. It's been one of my favorites since it came out."

"Mine, too." She tilted her head to the side and tucked her hair behind her ear again. Hand in hand, they walked to the mock dance floor arranged in the sanctuary.

As the song was ending, Jackie didn't want to let go.

Michal caressed the back of her hand with his thumb. "Jace, can we catch up over coffee? We could grab some fudge on the way."

"Sure, I'd really like that."

JACKIE SMILED AT THE MEMORIES from last Christmas. She looked up at Michal and whispered a silent prayer, thanking God for this wonderful gift of love and asking him to help her and Mick figure out a way to stay together and work on the mission field.

Michal took her hand. "And second," he said, "I'm sorry if I was short in our earlier conversation. I wanted to surprise you and was going to wait until after the party, but . . . I finished my flight hours and have almost completed my application for MAF. I just need to know what to put for my marital status."

Jackie gasped. "Seriously?"

He led her onto the dance floor as Phil Wickham sang "This Year for Christmas," the song they danced to a year ago. Jackie looked around to see Uncle Stu and some friends standing next to a large arch of red and white roses.

Was that arch there when I came in? Jackie's heart pounded like thunder. *Is this what I think it is? Is this for real?*

Michal reached into his pocket and pulled out a box. Then he took her left hand and bent down on one knee. She drew in a breath. He opened the box. "Jace, I love you. I'm so glad we found each other after so much time apart. This past year has been amazing, and I can't imagine my life without you. Will you change my status from single and marry me?"

Jackie took the box and admired the ring inside. She hesitated for a moment, then tears fell down her cheeks. She fumbled for the right words to say. "I—I don't know."

Michal stood and wrapped his hands around hers, still holding the box. "Jace, if this is about earlier, I truly am sorry."

A tear rolled down her cheek as she stared at their hands. "No, no. It's . . ." She wiped her cheek. "Have you spoken to my dad?"

"He sure has." A familiar voice came from behind Michal. Jackie looked up to see her dad walking toward them.

"Daddy!?" Jackie hugged him and sobbed. "Oh, Daddy!"

"Hey, baby girl!" Dad returned her hug and stroked her hair like he did when she was little.

Jackie pulled back. "Where's Mom?"

Jackie's mom joined the daddy-daughter hug. "I'm here, sweetie. We all wanted to surprise you for Christmas. We've been talking and planning for months."

Uncle Stu joined the family reunion. "Hi, Grace!" he said, hugging Jackie's mom. He gave Jackie's dad a handshake that turned into a hug.

Dad reached his hand toward Michal. "Mick, good to see you, son."

"Thank you, Mr. Harten. You as well."

Dad put his arm around Mom, smiled at Jackie, and nodded toward Michal. "So, are you going to leave him hanging?"

"Yes!—I mean, no. Ugh." Jackie turned to Michal. "Yes! I will marry you!" She handed him the box and held out her left hand.

Michal put the ring on Jackie's finger. Then he wrapped his arms around her, picked her up, and spun them both around. When he set her down, he kept one hand on her waist. With the other, he tucked her hair behind her ear, put his other hand on her face, and gently pulled her close. He bent down and softly touched his lips to hers. The scent of his body spray and the sweet aroma of fudge intoxicated her. She closed her eyes and welcomed his touch. Her heart raced as he pressed closer, giving her the perfect first kiss while their favorite Christmas music played.

Story Inspiration

"A Touch of Fudge and Romance" was inspired by my daughter, Adia Grace, stillborn at thirty-six gestation weeks on September 26, 2017. My husband and I adopted Isabella a year later. Had Adia lived, the two girls would celebrate the same birth year, born just three days apart. While watching Isabella dance and sing one day, I started dreaming about what Adia might be like and the life she might've had, and this anthology story was the result.

The characters Jackie and Grace were named in memory of my mother and my daughter, and Michal was named in memory of my father. I am currently working on a novel trilogy and plan to incorporate this story into that series.

I'm donating my proceeds from this anthology to Beautiful Gate Lesotho (beautifulgatelesotho.org).

About Mari

Mari Eygabroad and her husband, Bryan, serve in missions in Lesotho, Southern Africa. Bryan is a pilot with Mission Aviation Fellowship (MAF). Mari is a homeschooling mama to their two children, Matthias and Isabella. While Mari does some outside ministry, including manual therapy for friends and mentoring new missionaries, her primary focus is raising her children as disciples of Christ.

Mari published a nonfiction book for missionary wives in 2022 and its companion workbook in 2023. In *Living Uprooted*, Mari shares what she wished she would have known before moving overseas and how God provided for her family in times of trial. As a member of the Lady Lits, she developed an interest in writing fiction. She enjoys the challenge of telling a compelling story with a spiritual message.

At marieygabroad.com, you can subscribe to Mari's monthly newsletter.

Better Than Magic

by Susan Marie Graham

To: Twinkle <TWINKLEMNGDIR@NORTHPOLE.NP>
From: Dizzy <dizzy@northpole.np>
Dec 23 at 4:14 p.m.
Subject: **I QUIT**
To the Manager:

Please see attached my resignation letter effective immediately. Thank you for your attention to this matter.

Very truly yours,

Dizzy, Factory Mfg.

<attachment>

To: Dizzy <dizzy@northpole.np>

From: Twinkle <twinklemngdir@northpole.np>

Dec 23 at 4:15 p.m.

Re: **I QUIT**

??!!! Now?!! We've discussed this. I already explained it's out of my hands.

To: Twinkle <twinklemngdir@northpole.np>

From: Dizzy <dizzy@northpole.np>

Dec 23 at 4:16 p.m.

Re: Re: **I QUIT**

Hence the resignation.

To: Dizzy <dizzy@northpole.np>

From: Twinkle <twinklemngdir@northpole.np>

Dec 23 at 4:17 p.m.

Re: Re: Re: **I QUIT**

I will meet with you to discuss further. I can fit you in my schedule on Dec 26 around 10 a.m.

To: Twinkle <twinklemngdir@northpole.np>

From: Dizzy <dizzy@northpole.np>

Dec 23 at 4:18 p.m.

Re: Re: Re: Re: **I QUIT**

Again, please see attached.

To: Punky <punkyasst@northpole.np>
From: Twinkle <twinklemngdir@northpole.np>
Dec 23 at 4:19 p.m.
Fwd: Re: Re: Re: Re: **I QUIT**
We have a situation. See below. Can you talk to him?

To: Twinkle <twinklemngdir@northpole.np>
From: Punky <punkyasst@northpole.np>
Dec 23 at 4:20 p.m.
Re: Fwd: Re: Re: Re: Re: **I QUIT**
Already did. We're scrambling over here. Advise you notify B.R.
p.s. Send help!

There *was* no more help. Twinkle laid down his tablet and drummed fingers on his desk. Notify B.R.? Was Punky kidding? Acting on that would put the nail in Twinkle's coffin!

Let's think about this. He crossed an ankle over his knee, the jingling of the bells on his shoes annoyingly merry, and studied the platter of snickerdoodles on his desk, as if the answer could be found in a cinnamony stack of cookies. He scanned the detailed schedule covering the whiteboard on the wall across from where he sat. Dizzy quitting would put them behind, no doubt about that. Nobody worked faster than Dizzy.

The thought of what B.R. would say gave Twinkle a chill. Disappointing that icon of kindness and generosity would be crushing. Not to mention, Twinkle had campaigned for this management position long and hard—since about the Civil War. When Jolly finally retired a few years ago, it came down to Twinkle and Dizzy. Twinkle couldn't afford to flop.

He always got the job done, didn't he? Wasn't he the one who kept them *ahead* of schedule last year, got all the elves a nice bonus? They should be thanking him. They should all be grateful. Nobody did a better job, not even Jolly, and Jolly left some mighty big shoes to fill. Why, even when—

Twinkle snapped straight up in his seat.

Jolly!

He snatched up his tablet and started typing.

To: Jolly <jolly@gmail.com>

From: Twinkle <twinklemngdir@northpole.np>

Dec 23 at 4:50 p.m.

Subject: PROBLEM

Hello, Jolly! (See what I did there? LOL.) Long time no see. How are you enjoying Arizona?

I won't beat around the bush. I find myself in a dilemma. My top producer quit and we're falling behind. I don't have to tell you what a disaster this could be.

What would you do? Any advice is appreciated.

Fondly,

Twinkle

Although he bristled at the admission of helplessness, what choice did he have?

He hit Send.

Arizona. He checked the array of world clocks lining the wall. Jolly would be fast asleep. No use sitting here waiting for a reply.

That troublemaker Dizzy. Lately he'd been pushing his belief system on everybody else. Three times he'd accosted Twinkle in the hallways, demanding that they make changes, that Christmas was too mercenary, that it was up to them to resurrect the true spirit of

Christmas and set an example for the world to look up to. Well, who was Dizzy to decide what everybody else should be doing? Who was Dizzy to disrupt so many years of tradition? Why couldn't he keep all that spirit stuff to himself?

Twinkle detected a sour face coming on. Dizzy had been out to get him since they'd first vied for the leadership of the Toy Factory. The very day of Jolly's retirement party, Twinkle saw Dizzy from a distance, schmoozing up to B.R. over a platter of petit fours. Twinkle made sure to play up his own accomplishments till the minute the new manager was decided by the Office of Elfin Affairs. He had a perfect record. Why shouldn't he be proud? And he'd been in Toys decades longer than Dizzy anyway. Why shouldn't he have gotten the job? Dizzy was the one who ruined it for himself, really, with all his nagging about the "true meaning of Christmas."

Everything Twinkle did—every doll crafted, every puzzle piece cut—was an effort to one day realize his secret dream, the honor of riding with B.R. in the sleigh on Christmas Eve. Twinkle had always played like it was no big deal. But it really, truly was. And everybody knew it. Whoever was chosen to ride the sleigh was given a special golden star with his name on it, to place on the fifty-foot Official Christmas Tree in North Pole Square. It was a much-coveted honor. Like getting the gold jacket for the Pro Football Hall of Fame.

Twinkle's reverie was broken by a *ding*!

But the email he received wasn't from Jolly.

It was a forwarded message from Punky, with the panicky heading "LOOK AT THIS!!!" Twinkle drew a sharp breath.

Three more resignations. Looked like Dizzy was talking to the ranks again, and it didn't bode well.

Twinkle looked back at the world clocks. He had to do something besides wasting time sitting and thinking.

He leapt to his feet and stomped to the door, shoes jangling madly every time his feet hit the floor. Yanking the door open intensified the hammering and whirring and buzzing of elves' tools from the nearby Toy Factory.

Quit on me, will they? We'll see about that. One way or another, he'd get the schedule back on track, before this nonsense went any further. He'd make the toys himself if it came to it.

Punky was approaching from the opposite end of the hall, wobbling under two enormous platters of cookies, one perched in either hand. Signaling for his assistant to follow, Twinkle headed toward the Reindeer Room, where the elves took much-needed breaks every hour.

They met up before a table as long as the West Coast and littered with empty, crumb-filled plates, half-full mugs of coffee or hot chocolate, crumpled napkins. There were spills and messes all over.

Punky placed the platters on the table, releasing a *pffffffft* of air from the effort. "Thirty-sixth cookie run since yesterday." He set about brewing another pot of coffee, the utensils shivering in his trembling hands.

The mingled scents of coffee, chocolate, cinnamon, nutmeg, and vanilla were enough to send any elf into a blissful swoon, but Twinkle carefully removed the half-eaten macaroon clutched in Punky's hand.

"I thought you were doing Keto," he said gently but through gritted teeth. Punky was naturally a nervous sort, but the last thing Twinkle needed was his right-hand man hopped up on caffeine *and* sugar. "Time for some protein and a good dose of vegetables."

A handful of elves wandered in to descend on the new articles of sustenance, and Twinkle steered Punky out of their earshot.

"Check the Archives for any history of mutiny. Maybe we can find a solution there."

Punky's eyes bulged in horror, and he clutched at Twinkle's sleeve. "Mutiny? The elves would never!"

"I know, but it wouldn't hurt to check." And it would take mere minutes to run a scan through their upgraded Ultra-Supercomputer.

"Oh dear," Punky blubbered, clinging to Twinkle. "Oh, dear, dear!"

Twinkle peeled him away by the collar. "Don't fall apart on me now, Punky. There must be something there. This can't be the only time in Christmas history that delay occurred because of a . . . *misfortune*. Use some ingenuity, and stop with the sugar already." He batted away the cookie Punky was reaching for. "You know you can't handle it anymore. Go eat some salt." One drawback from transferring from the hustle and bustle of toymaking to the more sedentary role of administration was that you had to take it easier on the sugar.

Punky's mouth pressed into a tight line. He scurried away in the direction of the Elfmover, to be spirited away by the monorail to the Archive Room.

Twinkle spun and backtracked toward the Toy Room. His first order of business was to calm everybody down and make sure they kept up their pace to finish the toys.

A number of elves looked up from behind their worktables when he entered the Factory, but they quickly put their heads down and continued hammering and assembling.

Another collection of world clocks was grouped on the Toy Room wall. Here, their faces were cheery and encouraging—a man in the moon, happy daisies, trucks with big smiles, and a certain oft-celebrated mouse. Their smiles seemed like sneers to him.

A massive trolley appeared on its way toward the Loading Zone, overburdened with packages and propelled by eight elves huffing against its weight. They were already packing the sleigh! Time was running out for Twinkle. He had to nip this rebellion in the bud, whatever tactics he used.

Who but Dizzy should come ambling toward him, then? As if he had not a care in the world.

"I'm not here," he said to Twinkle. "I'm only heading to clean out my locker."

Twinkle forced a smile and turned to address the room.

"All right, listen up, crew. I know some of you have been subjected to the grumblings of certain malcontents." He held up a hand at the instant mutterings from the audience. "With good reason, mind you. I want you to know . . ." He placed a hand over his heart. ". . . your concerns are my concerns. Dizzy here has brought something very important to my attention."

He put an arm around Dizzy's shoulders. Ignoring the straightening of Dizzy's spine, Twinkle only held him tighter.

"In fact, Christmas next year will be entirely different. Punky and I have already been talking. We'll move up the toymaking schedule to allow us more time to focus on the true meaning of Christmas." He patted Dizzy's shoulder heartily.

Dizzy twisted away, one eyebrow furrowing into a skeptical quirk. "Since when?"

"I've been working on a plan to put before B.R. as soon as this season is over. Of course, there's no time to change anything now, but next year . . ." Twinkle trailed off, leaving the elves to come to their own conclusions. "And, of course, any suggestions are welcome."

"You said that last year." Dizzy folded his arms. An anonymous chorus followed.

"Yeah!"

"That's right!"

"He certainly did!"

Twinkle held up both hands in a pleading position. "Understand that toymaking is our *job*. It's what we *do*." Sweeping his gaze over the multitude of dubious faces, he delivered his coup de grâce.

"For the *kids*."

The cynical faces immediately softened. All the elves turned to one another, nodding and murmuring.

"The *kids*!"

"Ah, yes, the *kids*!"

"We must think of the *kids*!"

Dizzy waved his arms for silence. "I move that those of us intending to resign put it to a vote. Do we stay or do we go?"

"Yes, of course!" Twinkle bobbed his head. "Take a vote and let me know what you decide. In the meantime, I'll be thinking about the most efficient way we can implement a different schedule, so the *kids* are taken care of."

Twinkle smiled, not without a tinge of self-satisfaction, and slowly took a few backward steps before he turned and scooted out of the Toy Room. He rubbed his hands together in jubilance. Crisis averted!

He was of a mind to check in on Punky, but midway to the Elf-mover, where the east and west corridors crossed, he came to an abrupt halt. Propped on a pedestal before him was Mrs. C.'s latest creation, a detailed gingerbread Nativity. His stomach rumbled at its scrumptious aroma.

The display was quite a work of admirable quality. Mrs. C. had painstakingly assembled the scene with carefully carved blocks of gingerbread, pastel fondant clothing, hair and faces delicately piped with icing. Heaped-together gumdrops served as manger walls, and Baby Jesus rested atop a bed of string licorice standing in for straw. Everything was frosted with a sugar snow that sparkled like diamonds.

She was quite the master craftswoman, Mrs. C. And her creation gave him an idea.

He changed direction and hurried downstairs to the Elfmover. He'd go to the North Pole Bakery, where Mrs. C. directed the troop of elves providing all the snickerdoodles needed to fuel the season, as well as festive delectables like peppermint fudge and baklava to leave under Christmas trees the world over.

Aboard the Elfmover, he pressed the Bakery button. The glass-enclosed railcar kept him warm as it sped smoothly along the tracks through the falling snow.

At the Bakery, he found Mrs. C., resplendent in her special Christmas apron embroidered with glittery angels and dusted over with splotches of flour. She was overseeing a batch of cookies hot from the oven, and the mouthwatering smells encircling Twinkle made his stomach flip over itself with burbling. Peanut butter perfume teased at his pointed nose.

Mrs. C. broke into a bubbly grin when she spotted him. "Twinkle! You're just in time. I know peanut butter's your favorite."

Which was true, but despite the aroma, his stomach was in knots. He politely accepted a cookie from the tray she held out to him.

"Scrumptious as always," he remarked after a nibble. "Mrs. C., may I speak to you? I have a problem I think you could help me with."

Mrs. C. looked down at him (for Mrs. C. was very tall) while she wiped her hands on her apron. Her glasses sagged lower on her nose, and her forehead wrinkled. The wrinkles deepened and multiplied as Twinkle relayed his predicament.

"Oh, my goodness," she mused, her face a veritable study in sympathy, "that *is* a worry. We've never had any elves resign before."

Twinkle froze. A shudder coursed through his backbone as her words hit home. He couldn't be the elf who inspired a massive walkout. He couldn't go down in history as the Elf Who Ruined Christmas. He would do anything to prevent that.

"And how do you think I can help?" she asked.

Twinkle took a breath and plunged ahead. "Magic cookies."

Mrs. C. gave a little jump of her shoulders.

"Wouldn't you think," Twinkle went on while Mrs. C. removed her glasses and gave them a vigorous polish with her apron, "that a bit of elfin Magic might provide the impetus to get us back on schedule? That it might sway the workforce into seeing things my way?"

He met Mrs. C.'s steady gaze. "That is to say," he quickly amended, "the *right* way, the way that would best benefit the *kids*?"

Mrs. C. was the Keeper of the Magic, which had been used more and more sparingly over the decades. The increased sophistication and technological advancements of each generation had rendered it all but obsolete, and it would be far too easy for the Magic to fall into the wrong hands. Therefore, it was guarded jealously and practiced rarely, the benefit of the *kids* notwithstanding.

"Twinkle," Mrs. C. said presently, "you know how Nick and I view the Magic."

"Yes, certainly."

"You know that improper handling of elfin Magic can be very dangerous."

"But of course."

"And that using the Magic to compel people to do something they are not inclined to do can have serious consequences."

This gave Twinkle pause for thought, but only for a millisecond. "We wouldn't want to disappoint the *kids* is all I'm saying."

"Hmm." Mrs. C. regarded him for a longish moment before she gave him a resolute nod. "You *are* in a jam, after all. I do believe this calls for the Big Guns."

"You mean—"

"Not just cookies. Cream puffs." She winked at his confusion. "*Special* cream puffs."

"Ah!"

"And can we agree that Nick needn't know about this misadventure? We wouldn't want to add to his worries for the next two days."

"Goodness, no!" Twinkle wouldn't dream of running into Mr. C. and saying "You'll never guess what we did, B.R.!" Not that anyone would call him Big Red to his face.

Tickled three-and-a-half shades of pink, Twinkle boarded the Elfmover and headed back to the Factory. He would return to his office and enjoy a hot cup of coffee while he tended to his supply inventory and bills of lading. He would leave his worries behind, because no matter what the elves decided among themselves, the Magic would take care of it.

Midway, he gasped and mashed the Stop button. The Elfmover skidded to a stop, and Twinkle watched wide-eyed as a line of elves traipsed across the overhead glass tunnel, away from the Toy Factory. Were they leaving? Impossible!

He continued on and grabbed his tablet the moment he reached his office. While he was away, Jolly's email had responded automatically. "Sorry, on Christmas vacation." Rubbish! Who takes a vacation from retirement?

Before that notification, though, he'd received eighteen more resignations, six leaves of absence, and forty-two leaving-early-not-feeling-wells. Traitors! That would leave less than four hundred working elves at the Factory.

All Dizzy's fault. It was lucky for Dizzy that he quit, or Twinkle would've given him the heave-ho-ho-ho.

Twinkle sat back hard in his chair and placed a hand on his stomach. The rumblings he'd experienced earlier at the yummy scents of the season had been supplanted by something a little uncomfortable, a little belly-achy, a little not-so-good.

He had to keep busy, that was all. Industry first. There was a job to do. He arose and left his office again to look in on Punky's progress.

At the hallway crossroad, he was arrested once again by the gingerbread Nativity, its sheer loveliness bringing him to a standstill. The distinctive zing of the gingerbread scent made his nostrils twitch delightfully.

It seemed he stood there a long time. As he gazed on the confectionary scene, a curious sensation befell him, a flutter or a fidget inside. Oddly, a tear slipped from the corner of his eye. He didn't brush it away. Instead, he was filled with the desire to drop to his knees, hold his hands together, and bow his head. "I don't deserve to ask," he whispered, "but could you help me, please?"

He stood and looked around, feeling a little odd—almost silly, but not quite that. With no one around to question his unusual behavior, he went on his way to the Archive Room, shoes jingling with every step. All at once he knew what he had to do.

To: Santa <sclaus@northpole.np>
From: Twinkle <twinklemngdir@northpole.np>
Dec 24 at 6:00 p.m.
Subject: Personal
Dear Santa,

It is with a heavy heart that I must deliver some unsettling news. We have fallen behind in production and are unable to meet quota as planned. The books are available for viewing at your convenience.

Please understand this misfortune in no way reflects on the elves. They are a hardworking and loyal team, and it has been my joy to lead them in my tenure here. The errors resulting in the shortfall are mine alone.

Once you depart on your route, I shall tender my resignation forthwith. The North Pole deserves an elf with more established leadership fortitude. To that end, I remain,

Your most humble and obedient servant,

Twinkle

P.S. May I recommend Dizzy as the ideal candidate to replace me?

Twinkle proceeded to the Reindeer Room, which was standing-room only, the overflow of elves spilling out to the Toy Factory. The air was thick with anticipation. Twinkle had sent a blast memo to the elves that morning via text message, saying Mrs. C. would be providing a special Christmas Eve treat they wouldn't want to miss. No elf on the planet would turn down that offer, not even the mutineers.

Twinkle was in a strange state of excitement and anxiety. The merry faces of the world clocks mocked him, and several trolleys brimming with packages trundled past on the way to the loading dock. B.R. would be making an appearance in a mere matter of hours, and if not for the Magic, all would be lost.

Mrs. C. entered at last, followed by her band of Bakery elves, bearing long trays laden with fat, cream-stuffed puffs nestled in gaily printed paper cups. A low chorus of "Ooh" rippled through the room.

Twinkle stood at the front of the cavernous room, a jittery Punky beside him. Mrs. C. instructed her bevy of elves as they plunked down platter after platter on the long table. She favored Twinkle with a wink, which settled him somewhat, but the skittish squishiness in his stomach wasn't going anywhere until he was sure the Magic had done its job. Even though he'd come clean with Santa, he wished mightily for a miracle that would save them all.

Dizzy, of course, was first at the table, sniffing in suspicion, brow furrowed. "What's this? Something new? I've never seen these before."

But the other elves were oohing and aahing, always particularly excited over any unusual treats that popped up. Already helping themselves, they carefully cradled the cups and looked the puffs over admiringly.

"These cream puffs," Twinkle said in an announcer's voice, "are our special gift to you. I asked Mrs. C. to bake a reward for a job well done. I'm very proud of all of you!"

Hesitating their indulgence, the elves searched each other's faces. They all knew they hadn't met the schedule. None of them had ever seen B.R. in a grump, but if anything could disturb his relentless cheerfulness, not finishing the toys would do it.

Seeing their worry made something flutter inside Twinkle. He stood straighter, a little startled that he really *did* feel proud. "It doesn't matter that we fell behind. I should've listened to Dizzy and addressed his concerns." He put a hand on Dizzy's shoulder. "I'm sorry. It was my fault, and I'll explain that to B.R. After Christmas, we'll make some changes around here. For now, everyone enjoy these special treats."

Dizzy stared open-mouthed at him. Twinkle just smiled back, his heart swelling. It felt good to say something nice. But he was astonished when Dizzy's eyes filled with tears.

"Why, Twinkle," Dizzy said, "you've become what I prayed for!"

Twinkle stood agape. "You prayed? For me?"

"Of course!" Dizzy wiped his eyes. "You were so unhappy in your job after wanting it for so long. It made me awfully sad. I prayed God would show you a better way, but I suppose I did try to rush it a little. Instead of quitting, I should've waited for him to come through. I suppose I could've been nicer. I'm sorry too."

The elves broke into hearty cheers as the two former rivals shook hands. Everyone smacked their lips over the sweet puffs. Dizzy grinned as he chewed. Twinkle selected a cream puff for himself and gave one to Punky, who'd been too flummoxed over the goings-on to grab his own.

As Twinkle savored the creamy goodness, he waited for the Magic to overtake him. But there wasn't a twinge or a twitch. Just a mouthful of blissful deliciousness.

"Ho, ho, ho!" came a bellow from behind, and the Jolly Old Soul himself appeared.

The elves cheered as Santa placed a kiss on Mrs. C.'s cheek, making her turn a pretty pink. Then he faced Twinkle, and the room fell quiet.

Twinkle braced himself for the worst. He certainly had it coming.

But Santa astounded him with a smile. "It takes an elf with a big heart to own up to his mistakes. How would you like to ride with me tonight?"

The sleigh ride! Twinkle's dearest wish! But he couldn't resist protesting under the circumstances. "The schedule fell so far behind. No amount of work will catch us up."

All eyes turned on Santa, who guffawed. "Schedule schmedule! We have enough backstock to cover this year and half of the next! Finish loading 'er up, boys! We have deliveries to make!"

Twinkle gawked at him. *Backstock?* He had no idea there was backstock. He was diligent about inventory and certain no backstock had accumulated.

The Magic! It worked!

While the buzzing of congratulations assailed Twinkle from all sides, a warm sensation enveloped him. He turned to find Dizzy and pulled him forward. "Santa, this is the elf you should reward. He has the biggest heart of all. If it hadn't been for him, I may never have realized what a toad I've been."

Santa leaned back and gave a hearty hoot of laughter. "Well, get a move on, Dizzy! Time's a-wasting!" He leaned forward (for Santa was even taller than Mrs. C.) and gave Twinkle a friendly elbow jab. "Never say B.R. isn't a good sport!"

A flood of elves surrounded a flabbergasted Dizzy, and Twinkle watched, cheeks burning, as they carried his new friend out to the sleigh, a chuckling Santa following.

Twinkle was strangely at peace. He'd never been so happy. As he headed out into the cold North Pole air, he paused in front of Mrs. C.

"Thank you," he breathed.

"And what are you thanking me for?" she asked.

"Why, the Magic, of course!" *Did she forget?*

Mrs. C. gazed at him fondly. "Twinkle, there's no Magic in the puffs. Everything that happened came from inside you. That's called Faith, and it's better than Magic."

Surprised into muteness, Twinkle stood dumbfounded as Mrs. C. left the Toy Factory.

At the stroke of midnight, he stood outside and watched with the other elves as the prancing reindeer hoisted the sleigh into the dark, star-sprinkled sky. His heart lifted along with it. *What a marvelous Christmas this is!*

Santa's sleigh grew smaller and smaller as it rose higher and higher, and there appeared a star in the eastern sky, brighter than any star Twinkle had ever seen. The reindeer steered the sleigh around it, once, twice, the rails of the sleigh casting a majestic glimmer before gliding the passengers and presents off and out of sight. The star winked at Twinkle—he was very sure.

Now that *was* Magic!

Story Inspiration

When the Lady Lits decided to write a book of Christmas stories, I wanted to touch on the magic of the holiday but somehow keep a focus on Jesus. And I wanted my story to be fun to read! I wondered, first, what elves would do if they were under the gun to meet their schedule and, second, what exactly might spark a schedule-upending rebellion within their ranks. Also, I'm a P. G. Wodehouse wannabe. I'm donating my proceeds from this anthology to Save the Storks (savethestorks.com), for the *kids*.

About Susan

Susan Marie Graham writes stories that explore the Christian experience in our fallen world, in both historical and contemporary settings. Her interest in vintage movies and World War II inspired her first novel, *There Will Your Heart Be*. Susan has been writing since she was ten but first thought of it as a career after she quit her corporate job and moved alongside the Great Smoky Mountains in Tennessee, where she enjoys life with her husband, their son, and the temperamentally affectionate cat Patches.

Discover more about Susan and her writing at susanmariegraham .com.

An Innkeeper's Wife

by J. Bea Wilson

Sophie smirks at the dough. The last-minute request from the Sisters to accommodate a gluten-free sweet tooth leaves no time for practice batches. This recipe has to work on the first try.

Doubt flares when the heavy mixture plops onto the parchment like poo. No elasticity. The lip she's chewing on may prove more appetizing. If only bowing out of the kitchen was an option for an innkeeper's wife.

Damp fingers help shape the tacky dough into neat rounds more to her liking. Her cheeks heat up again over Sister Angelica's earlier comment to Father Mark. "Sophie worships by creating simple confections of the highest order. No special need will trouble her."

"I mind a little," she mutters now. Carrying Gran's loaded biscuit sheets to the oven, she feels the weight of being the inn's sole chef.

Whipping up treats *is* in her wheelhouse. But no wheat flour? She might as well bake with both thumbs knotted in her apron strings. Gluten substitutes don't grow in the inn's garden, and her teff flour is for flatbread, not biscuits.

Still, she doesn't regret saying "Will do." What would become of the inn if the Nevada chapter of the Sisters of Peaceful Mind didn't rent the whole establishment every Christmas Eve, keeping its budget out of the red for the first quarter? In their mission to provide uplifting getaways for folks experiencing difficult circumstances, the Sisters are extending charity to her and Sam as well. Any time Sophie forgets that, her husband's delight in running the inn reminds her.

Cradling a throbbing forehead in one palm, she uses her other pinky finger to capture an amber drip from the leaf-shaped bottle of maple syrup on the counter. Its sweetness on her tongue sends her thoughts half a world away and a decade backward. Eyes closed, she's in Gran's New Zealand kitchen, having Kiwi wisdom poked into her ribs with the end of a rolling pin.

"If the ingredients are good, the mix will be too."

The phantom pain in Sophie's side contributes to a lump forming in her throat. The tears are backing up again. Since last week's "definitive diagnosis," it's been impossible to allay them more than a few hours. Today has to be different. No crying in front of guests.

Swallowing hard, she paws open the oven door with the mitts her best friend crocheted for her in holiday green. As usual, Vi knew just the right words of wry encouragement to hand over with the flannel-lined gloves. "We're in this together. I used your catchphrase to compensate for rendering fingers useless."

Despite the intoxicating smell of warming chocolate, Sophie wrinkles her nose at the self-proclaimed motto embroidered with ropy red yarn: "Be" on the left mitt, "Kind" on the right, more succinct than the Maori proverb "If kindness is sown, then kindness you shall receive." How did Vi manage to point a prescient finger at today's struggle over biscuits?

"Not 'biscuits,'" Vi would say. "Cookies." For the sake of the inn's guests, Vi is on a crusade to impress Americanisms into Sophie's vocabulary of British English. "Friends in need"—isn't that the Sisters' motto? Vi would bristle at identification with the Sisters but lives that creed without effort.

After finagling Gran's *cookie* sheets out of the beeping oven and onto a cooling rack, Sophie tosses the mitts on the counter and puts one hand over her heart, mustering enthusiasm for her allergic guest.

"Made this just for you!" she says, forcing a smile and dipping the thumb of her other hand into a ceramic bowl of warm water.

She pokes her thumb into balls of dough just as deep brown, jerking it out each time she feels the burn. A few balls in, she lets out a held breath. The dimples left in her thumb's wake confirm the recipe's success.

"Your joy is my joy!" she sings on repeat, spooning a generous half teaspoon of her prickly pear jam into each well and returning the sheets to the oven. Being asked to offer encouragement while in her own season of loss is good irony. Maybe she'll join the Sisters' order if, God forbid, something ever happens to Sam.

She stores her cocoa, salt, and baking powder in the cabinet he built her. A layer of dust taunts her into passing a tea towel across the front edge of each shelf. The attention calls to mind the cabinet's former life as a crate Gran shipped to the U.S. when Sam and Sophie extended their mission trip indefinitely.

Twelve seasons of Christmas guests aren't the inn's only occupants yearning for traditions interrupted by circumstances. Sophie believes in the mission they accepted, but just a minute barbecuing under a pohutukawa tree back in the homeland would soothe her.

The next best thing is remembering the shine on Sam's face when he unveiled the finished cabinet, like when he mooned over plates of biscuits she set on Gran's rimu table when they were courting. Her face still reddens every time he says "Nobody bakes like Sophie!"

When the timer chimes again, she shuffles the fully baked cookies onto cooling racks with her lucky spatula, the pitted one left to her by Sam's mother. Sophie takes a deep breath of expectation. Sam will praise her baking again for the millionth time when the guests arrive in—

A punch to the timer button resets the oven's digital display to clock. Uh-oh! Two hours. She strips off her baking apron and slips into her cleaning one with a soft tsk.

Sam doesn't brag on her housework, at least not her timing of it. But her baked goods, jams, and syrups make up for that weakness. Besides, she always pulls through in the end.

Just when she tucks away her cleaning supplies almost two hours later, there's a familiar pattern of raps at the back door. It's too early for Harold to pilfer a leftover plate of cookies for the guests at his B&B. When she cracks open the door, the strain on her older brother's face migrates to hers as she assesses the couple shifting foot to foot behind him. Their tired clothing needs a wash, and the young man's cheeks are pink as bing cherries.

"*Kia ora*, Soph," Harold says, looking past her. "Where's Sam?" She presses her lips together. It's the question Harold usually asks when he needs a favor, ever ready to imply that Sam's heart is softer than hers.

"The barn prob'ly." A shiver travels down her spine from the cool air descending over the desert valley with nightfall. Should she invite these people in? Her expected guests will arrive any minute. "What's up?"

"These loves are lookin' to pass the night, and my place is chocka."

Sophie glances at Harold's quiet B&B across the street, then frowns. "Y'know all our rooms are let for Christmas."

"Yeah, but . . ." The view Sophie gets when Harold steps aside delivers a sock to her diaphragm. Pregnant. This olive-skinned girl must've been in diapers when Sophie first started trying. The young man lays a protective hand over the girl's swollen belly. Sophie reels aside to let Harold escort them into the kitchen.

Sam trails in behind them with a whoop. "Might be in for a cool night," he says. "Howdy! I'm Sam." He shakes hands with the couple and flashes a toothy smile.

His eyes cloud over when they meet Sophie's, and he reaches a hand toward her as if she's a china doll about to fall off a shelf. She takes the cue to rearrange her face and paste on a smile.

"Would you believe he goes by Joseph and her by Mary?" Harold asks with a sheepish grin.

"As in Merry Christmas, though." The girl wraps a strand of straight dark hair around one finger. Her laugh is shy but melodious.

"You can call me Joe," the young man says, his blue eyes following the sound of footsteps in the front hall as Harold repeats the couple's dilemma.

"We'll work something out." Sam winks at Sophie's subtle head-shake. "After we settle our other guests."

She follows him to the hall with labeled plates of cookies and ushers their first arrivals to the cozy dining nook off the kitchen, serving hot cocoa and peppermint tea while Sam thanks the military parents for their only son's service and regrets that their boy is overseas on the holiday. Sam invites the mother to have a cut-out angel cookie dusted in powdered sugar.

The short round woman teases Sophie for her thinness. "Only if you join me."

Sophie knows her gluten angels are sound. She munches on a gluten-free jammed thumb instead with raised eyebrows. Not half bad.

It's no surprise to find Harold and her other gluten-free plate gone when she and Sam return to the young couple in the kitchen. *Serves his thievin' self right if his guests don't like 'em.*

Sam jerks his head in the direction of the barn. She grits her teeth and nods. When he first suggested his notion of a rustic hideaway, all she said was "Who'll wanna stay with Bessy and the goats?" Now, it's as if his recent eagerness with the hammer nailed this emergency. Vi would say beggars can't be choosers anyway.

Before Sam can offer the barn room to Joe and Merry, new voices call the innkeepers back to the hall, to greet the couple recently displaced by a house fire, followed by the gaunt mother whose daughter has lain comatose in the hospital for six months. Sophie's heart sinks to her toes at the weariness in the mother's eyes. What's harder? Being unable to have children, like her and Vi? Or watching your child suffer?

Why, God? Sophie pleads. No answer is no surprise. Though one might expect this day to be different.

"Made this just for you," Sophie says to the single mom, offering her a jammed thumb.

The mother smiles gratitude around a gluten-free mouthful. Delight pushes the weariness from her eyes and unsettles Sophie, willing to mourn for both of them. *Your sorrow is my sorrow.*

Dispersing her own clouds of sadness before they drop a downpour, Sophie follows Christmas Eve protocol like a well-programmed AI. A fresh platter of gluten cookies. More warm drinks. A cheerful escort to rooms decorated with garland, strings of dimmable colored lights, and themed Christmas trees.

With all official guests settling in before the evening's dinner and entertainment, she leads Joe and Merry to the barn by lanternlight. Inside the walled-off guest room, she sets the evening's last plate of angel cookies on the tiny dining table Sam fashioned from an industrial cable spool. "Rustic chic," he called it. Then she opens the valve on the radiator and sniffs the air.

"I hope you'll find the lingering barn smells tolerable."

Merry waves away Sophie's concern and subsequent apology for the in-progress decor. Pregnant, young, and carefree, Merry is Sophie's antithesis.

"Exactly how far along are you?" Sophie asks, pulling extra pillows from the dented steamer trunk serving as one of the little room's two seats.

"Oh, no worries!" Merry clutches a pillow with a crocheted cover, Vi's handiwork. "My midwife says I'm not due for two weeks."

Sophie closes her eyes rather than roll them. "My Gran was a midwife." She bites back Gran's oversight of more deliveries early than on time and stares at the cookies on the spool table. Not the healthiest fare for an expecting mother.

"Those look delicious, Miz Sophie, but—"

Sophie's shoulders tighten at the girl's twisting smile.

"It's just that I can't eat gluten, for medical reasons."

"Yeah, thanks, Missus," Joe adds with a somber nod, "but you should save those for your guests in the inn." He shakes his head of blond curls. "We don't wanna be no trouble."

The tempered-glass plate feels heavy as wrought iron as Sophie carries it back to the inn. This morning, she'd never even heard of gluten freedom. Suddenly, people are proclaiming it all around her, tainting her satisfaction with her signature angels.

Sitting by the warm brick hearth amid the guests two hours later, she fights to keep heavy eyelids open as Father Mark's baritone drones the Christmas story. She jerks against Sam's side when the priest shouts "Freedom!"

She doesn't remember him going on so in years past. Baby Jesus this, Baby Jesus that. Baby, baby, baby.

"Where would we be without that baby?" His question hangs in the air.

In the solemn silence that awaits answer, there's a soft whimper. Sam laces his fingers with Sophie's, and she gasps, then flushes. The whimper came from her.

Father Mark covers their joined brown hands with his pale one. "Let us pray."

Pray. Why? Seems that's all she and Sam—and she and Vi—have done for years, to no avail. "In God's good time," Sam always says in place of amen.

According to modern medicine, Sophie's time is never. The slight movement of Sam's lips as Father Mark recites his usual Christmas prayer hypnotizes her into finally dropping her eyes closed. She can't open them, even when she hears the guests shuffling around her. Then a sudden cool breeze snaps her to attention, betraying Merry and Joe as they slip into the inn to join the caroling around the Nativity.

Witnessing Merry weep quietly through "Ave Maria" shoves Sophie into a penitent mood. The Sisters' cracking voices are enough to make any listener cry. But Merry's bowed head and hand over her abdomen speak a gratitude broad for the girl's years. For the first time in a decade, Sophie notices the Sisters' lifted chins, their beseeching eyes, the joy radiating from their faces as they sing. Pure joy from having hearts fixed on God alone.

From the kitchen door, Sophie watches Joe and Merry's slow walk to the barn after the festive evening draws to a close. The fingers of their laughter begin to free her from the straitjacket of envy. She smiles at Merry's squeal when Joe attempts and fails to lift her over the barn door's threshold.

Since worries ping-ponging between her ears won't let her sleep, Sophie pulls a fresh batch of gluten-free jammed thumbs from the oven at 12:01 a.m. Thinking of presenting them to Joe and Merry after sunrise, she glances through the kitchen window. Light escaping a wide crack at the top of the barn door casts a glistening pool on the sand in the dooryard. If the young couple is awake, they could probably use a snack.

That this intrusion may be a bad idea occurs to her on the dirt path. Her soft knock is met by rustling from inside.

"Wait!" Joe yells. *Definitely a bad idea.*

"I'm sorry to bother," she says when he throws open the door. "Made this just for—"

His darting eyes and labored breathing guide her thoughts to the one thing that could inspire his apparent panic.

"The baby?"

His head, neck, and shoulders bob. "Coming!!!"

She invites herself in. At the sleigh bed waiting for a refinish, Merry wraps fingers around Sophie's wrist like a handcuff. "Help!"

"Shhh, we got this, love."

Do they? A quick look under Merry's peasant skirt confirms there's no time to get to the hospital. This baby is coming now—thankfully headfirst. Joe heels to the commands Sophie barks.

She hasn't been this close to a human birth since Gran delivered little sister Mia. But time folds in the barn like a swaddling blanket. Every move Sophie saw Gran make flows through her hands.

"Merry Christmas!" she says, laying a baby boy in a breathless Merry's arms.

Sophie had forgotten about parents' first exaltations. Wondrous grunts. Huffs of joy. Otherworldly giggles. She waits a good ten minutes before cutting the cord with a pair of shearing scissors Joe sterilized in a pot of boiling water on the woodstove.

Soon thereafter Joe plops down at the spool table and eyes the jammed thumbs. "I'm starving!"

"A gluten-free recipe," Sophie says. "May become a favorite." Something about gazing at a newborn baby opens the heart to all possibilities.

Joe lifts a cookie high. "A perfect way to celebrate!"

"They're just biscuits," Sophie says with a chuckle.

"The *perfect* biscuits! Right, Merry?"

He returns to the sleigh and wraps his fingers around the hand Merry holds against her lips. She nods and blinks tears down her cheeks, though her other hand protests the cookie he offers.

"A new mom is frequently nauseous," Sophie explains.

He chews happily. "Mmm, still perfect, since avoiding gluten helped Merry get preggers."

Sophie's mouth works without sound. Merry beams, eyes wide. "Are you celiac too, Miz Sophie?"

"Am I—?" Sophie notices the scrambled state of the little room and starts tidying. "No! No, I—" Had she heard that word before? Her tongue trips over a conviction in her spirit. "What is—? How do you spell that?"

"C-e-l-i-a-c." Merry's voice slurs with fatigue.

Sophie slides Vi's crocheted pillow behind the new mother's head and accepts the drowsy baby back into her arms. Should she look into this celiac thing? Dare she hope again? Now? After the doc put a pin in her infertile womb?

Vi always says God steps in when he's our only hope.

Sophie is counting little olive toes and fingers for the umpteenth time when Sam appears in the barn's doorway. His look of concern gives way to wonder at finding her cradling a baby boy while the spent new parents sleep.

"Meet Jesse."

An ear-to-ear grin splits Sam's face. "*Ka Pai*, Soph!!! Well done!"

After staring at the baby with her for several minutes, he grabs a jammed thumb from the table, then another. "These jammies are different. Your recipes just keep getting better."

He kneels beside her seat on the steamer trunk by the bed and looks up at her like she's Wonder Woman. "Nobody bakes like my Sophie."

She blushes at his pleasure, longs to see his black eyes and bright smile in a tiny brown face. But she's been so hard toward God lately. Why would he help her now?

Her gaze returns to Jesse's fluttering eyelids. His eyes open, and she hears the Father's voice.

Made this just for you.

Her heartbeat skips. She's just hearing things, hearing what she wants to. He speaks again, with a steady voice that doesn't touch the eardrums but reverberates in the chambers of her heart.

Daughter, I made this just for you.

She studies Sam's adoring eyes. Did he hear the voice too? He rests his forehead on her knees, drawing her eyes back to Jesse's. The baby's face blurs.

What exactly is this, Abba? Are you saying there's a chance for me to—?

She blinks away her tears, then reaches out one arm to lay a hand across Merry's cool forehead. *Or are you calling me to a new mission?*

Merry sighs in her sleep. Joe snores beside her. Jesse puckers his pink lips.

Sam stretches out on the distressed wood he used to construct his barn hideaway's floor and grins up at them all.

Sophie smiles at the child.

Story Inspiration

Since I have multiple food allergies, I loved leaning into the challenge and opportunity of contributing to an anthology including holiday recipes. I hope Sophie's story encourages folks struggling to relate to their own or others' allergies or discouragements in a season when food and light hearts are so integral to fellowship. It was great fun to write a story featuring Sophie, Sam, and Vi, supporting characters in a novel en route to publication, recasting the Genesis account of Leah into the 2000s and exploring questions of disability and disappointment.

I'm donating my anthology proceeds to Joni and Friends (joniandfriends.org).

About J. Bea

JILL "J. BEA" WILSON joyfully adopted her pen name after living with chronic pain for more than twenty years. With the support of her husband, Brian, and the companionship of their rescue chihuahua, Bilbo, she is embracing her season of knitting wooly yarns, fiber and fiction. She is excited to be writing a series recasting biblical accounts into modern and future contexts. Her storytelling encourages readers that God's strength lifts people with disability to the benefit of the whole body of Christ.

To join J. Bea's *Lift!* community, lifting hearts and hands through story, visit jbeawilson.com.

The Greatest Gifts

by Janet Joanou Weiner

PARIS, DECEMBER 25, 1991

In the early morning hours, they came. Pangs and tightenings increased until it became obvious. Our baby was on the way, right on her due date.

Throughout the previous evening, internal shifts and rumblings had alerted me the time was approaching. Determined to make our Christmas Eve meal, I'd cooked for most of the twenty-fourth, including coffee cake for the next morning and a creamy shrimp dip for later on Christmas Day, my mom's recipe, poured into the curved copper fish mold she'd given me.

As is traditional in France, we'd gathered around the table for the *réveillon*, a long Christmas Eve meal of festive foods. While I lay awake, timing contractions in the predawn of Christmas morning, gratitude filled my heart. *You got me through all that cooking. And then allowed my family to be together for dinner. A gift. Thank you, Lord.* We'd even managed a family portrait, thanks to a camera with a timer on a tripod.

I'd planned for our other children's births not to be near Christmas. My birthday is in May, and I've always appreciated celebrating (and receiving presents!) in another part of the year. However, this fourth child set her own course from the beginning. Her due date was not just *near* Christmas. It was on the very day. The twenty-fifth of December. Today.

Still cozy in bed, I took in the digital clock's display. 5:30 a.m. No light seeped through the cracks of the shuttered window. All was calm and relatively silent for Paris. Another contraction gripped my abdomen.

After it subsided, I nudged my husband awake. "Dudley!"

"Hmm?" He rolled toward me, still half asleep.

"Merry Christmas!"

"Uh, Merry Christmas."

"So, I've been having contractions for a few hours now. They're not letting up. Maybe growing stronger."

He bolted up and threw off the covers. "Okay. You think it's time?" He blinked away remnants of sleepiness and stood poised, ready for action.

We stared at each other for a moment. Our last two children were born within four hours, from start to finish. The drive to the Parisian birth clinic was about twenty minutes if traffic didn't interfere, which it most likely wouldn't on Christmas morning.

"Well, they're not painful yet. I think we can wait here awhile."

"Okay, if you're sure."

"Yes, I'll let you know when it's time to go. Let's wake the kids to open presents."

"They'll love that!"

We both chuckled. For once, we were the first to rise on Christmas morning.

After another contraction, I followed him to the children's room.

Dudley leaned over their beds, stroking their backs. "Wake up! Let's have Christmas!"

They looked confused. I could see their sleepy brains processing. *It's still dark outside. Mom and Dad never wake us up this early.* Their pause lasted all of three seconds.

Christmas-morning excitement raced through their bodies, and they hopped out of bed, wondering what awaited them in the living room. They pulled on robes and slippers, following our tradition of staying in the bedroom until called out. Dudley made hot chocolate that no one drank. I made myself as comfortable as possible on the couch.

Dudley started the Charlie Brown Christmas music, and we gave the kids the go-ahead. They ran to the living room with shouts of glee, which I hoped didn't disturb the neighbors in our building.

Sharing the kids' joy through increasing contractions, I was thrilled when Josh saw his new bike and when Jessica and Hannah discovered the dollhouse Dudley built for them. Once we'd tucked them in bed the night before, surely with visions of all kinds of good things dancing through their heads, he'd brought these significant gifts up from our basement. I'd placed doll furniture inside the amazing three-story house, complete with a balcony terrace. I might've played a little myself.

Adjusting my pillows on the couch, I remembered the moment last night when I'd finished setting everything up and lumbered to my feet from the floor. The baby descended then, a significant pull. Deep breaths and stretches eased the discomfort. I'd thought the shift was likely from cooking all day and sitting too long on the hardwood floor. Another wave of gratitude had washed through me—I'd made it through getting the dollhouse ready. *Oh Lord, I'd love to be here when they first see it in the morning.*

And I was. The girls squealed and got right to enjoying the dollhouse. Josh yelled "cool" and tried to ride the bike around the not-so-big apartment, until Dudley promised to take him outside for a proper spin later.

Another contraction gripped my abdomen, increasing in pain and lasting longer. Staring at the quilted wreath hanging nearby, I drew deep breaths through my nose, then blew them out my mouth in soft puffs, trying not to draw attention to my laboring. As the contraction dissipated, I refocused my gaze on the kids and smiled. *Thank you, Lord, that I'm here to experience all this—such a gift.*

The children unpacked their Christmas stockings, bringing items (that I'd bought) to the couch for me to see. The excitement of the day—and the presents—absorbed all their attention. None of them questioned my lying on the couch, occasionally staring into the distance and breathing rhythmically.

As contractions grew even longer in duration and closer together, the time drew near for us to leave. Christmas with my family, at least in the traditional sense, was almost over. I took a moment and looked around the living room, setting it in my mind like a photograph.

Our apartment-sized Christmas tree, filled with traditional ornaments made or collected over the years, brought to mind a day earlier in December. The family doctor who checked on Josh's flu with a house call (yes! so nice!) had stopped to inspect the tree, which barely reached his chest. "Very pretty," he announced after a moment. "So English."

"*Merci*," I responded, surprised. "Thank you. But you know we're American."

"*Oui.* Yes, but this is very English."

I'd thought about that response after he left. Maybe our American Christmas aesthetic originally came from England, the Charles Dickens version of the holiday. The French's very different, more modern style included lots of blue and purple decorations. My taste ran toward red and green, *the* Christmas colors. Or so I'd thought. There's no international rulebook for the holiday. Why not purple and blue?

Around 7:00 a.m., we decided it was time to go to the hospital. While Dudley ran several blocks to where he'd last parked our orange VW van, I kept my vigil on the couch, watching the kids play and interacting with them as much as possible. Nostalgia gripped my chest, interrupted by the clutching in my uterus.

Dudley drove back to our building, double-parked, then ran upstairs to help me to the car. Joseph, a very kind single friend, arrived to stay with the kids. We'd expected the children to be sad to part with us on this day of all days. When they barely looked up from their gifts to say goodbye, we laughed and left, reassured they were fine.

Off we drove to a funky birthing clinic on the outskirts of Paris. I'd chosen it because they employed natural childbirth methods, practically unheard of then in France. Our third child was born in an ancient hospital in the French Alps, built in the time of Napoleon. Unfortunately, the approach of its nurses matched the sadly outdated facilities. I'd been relieved to find this Parisian clinic that encouraged parents to give input and make decisions throughout the birth. Best of all, unlike most French hospitals, this one allowed visits from siblings.

Known for facilitating underwater births, the center featured a massive hot tub in each room. Although I didn't plan to have a water birth, I found the warm bath helpful during parts of labor.

Stuck off to the side, behind the tub and next to a large window, the room's bed was almost an afterthought. Through labor pains, I looked out from it at apartment buildings, imagining Christmas happening inside them. While celebrations took place among families across the world, I was in a universe of my own, definitely experiencing a unique Christmas for me. Pangs of missing my children and the blessing of a normal (and pain-free) holiday blended with awareness of the miracle of new life.

After hours of contractions with insufficient progress, with the process taking much longer than my last births, two more midwives joined the one already attending me. Eventually, it was birth time, and our baby emerged. Halfway.

"STOP!" All three midwives looked at me from the foot of the delivery bed, speaking over each other in urgent tones. Dudley's body tensed.

"*Pas de panique*," said one, holding up a hand, her face lined with concern. "Don't panic," she restated in English.

I got it the first time. A myriad of thoughts raced through my head. *You've got to be kidding me. STOP now? The most painful moment in the whole process? And I'm not panicking. YOU ARE. What's happening?*

Agitation on their faces, plus a heightened level of intensity, conveyed something was wrong. I heard mumbled words about the cord around the baby's neck, about cutting it loose. Dudley leaned over my bottom half farther, watching every move. I barely had time to take all this in, then our daughter was born.

Sarah Ruth emerged slightly blue. But as a midwife held her up, Sarah gulped huge breaths of air and pinked up immediately, a warrior in nature.

Dudley hooted and hollered. He filled me in on the lead midwife's swift actions from moments before—cutting the cord, unwrapping it, and releasing our baby into the world.

"Is she going to be okay?" I asked the midwife who put Sarah on my chest. My voice wobbled as my body flooded with relief that the birth was over, plus an overwhelming love for the warm little being in my arms.

"She'll be just fine," the midwife said, her voice firm.

I wondered how she could be sure so soon, but reassurances from the three midwives that all was well with Sarah proved true. At eight pounds and some ounces, she was our biggest baby and by far the largest in a clinic filled with tiny French newborns. She nursed well, and her robust cries assured us she could make her voice heard.

Dudley returned home and later brought the children to meet their new sister. They walked into my room wearing clothes I'd never seen, clutching a new doll or book, the girls sporting hair ribbons I hadn't bought—Christmas gifts sent from Grandma and Grandpa, aunts and uncles. It was a little surreal for me not to have been part of the receiving process, also slightly comical to find they had no idea who gave them what. That year, our relatives received generic notes—"Thank you for the gifts"—as the kids hadn't paid attention to words past their own name on any tag.

I asked how their morning went, hoping to hear their Christmas had been nice despite us not being there for most of it. "Everything went okay with Joseph? You guys had fun?"

"Yeah, it was fun. But it was over way too fast!"

"We all opened our presents at the same time. No one stopped us."

"I never want to do it that way again."

"I like watching everyone else open their presents."

"Yeah, I'm glad you make us take turns and wait for each other."

My heart filled with warmth. The children learned that receiving their own presents was only part of the fun. Besides not wanting the revelry to be over quickly, they'd discovered that a great deal of the blessing comes from sharing in the joy of others—an unexpected gift of understanding on this highly unusual Christmas day.

There was more. The sea of wrapping paper, up to the kids' shins in our small living room, had caught their attention.

"It was a mess!"

"No one threw away the wrapping paper."

"It was everywhere."

"I like it best when you're there and keep everything picked up."

I smiled over the lessons taught by this unique Christmas.

The children crowded around my bed, eyes wide, ready for a turn holding Sarah. Josh, the experienced big brother at age ten, went first. *Thank you, Lord, they are here! Such a gift that they are allowed in the clinic to meet and hold their new baby sister on the day of her birth.*

Later in the evening, with Dudley and the children snug at home and with Sarah in the nursery for a bit, I made my way to the second-floor pay phone. Dudley had contacted family earlier, but loneliness engulfed me, and I needed to connect with my parents. Finally, after several tries, many coins, and a necessary reversal of charges, my long-distance call to California went through.

With celebratory Christmas noises behind him, Dad remarked on the uniqueness of my giving birth on Christmas. "Like Mary and, you know, like Jesus. It's a gift." Tears rose, and my throat tightened with gratitude as I thought of the day's greatest gifts—along with a hefty dose of homesickness.

After hanging up, I retraced my steps through the dim hallway to my room. With Baby Sarah in my arms again, my loneliness faded away. When I called her name, she opened her eyes and looked right at me, her intense gaze reminding me of something. *Oh! My* eyes. The shape, the hint of hazel-green to be. Even the way she studied me. My soul filled with peace. *She's here, she's safe, and she's incredibly precious. Thank you, Lord.*

While I'd never intended to give a child a birthday in competition with such a special holiday, her arrival signified the miraculous gift of *life* given to me twice over. First through Jesus, born to secure life forever with him. Then through Sarah Ruth, our beautiful warrior princess, born on Christmas Day.

Story Inspiration

I grew up in a family where Christmas was highly celebrated. My mom made a lovely big deal of the holiday. The kids dressed up for photos with Santa Claus at the local department store and baked and decorated sugar cookies. Our family showed up early for the Christmas Eve candlelight service. All the festivities culminated in Christmas Day, when the children ran from our bedrooms to the Christmas tree at our parents' signal to see what "Santa" brought and to check if he'd eaten the cookies and eggnog left out for him. Later, grandparents, aunts, and uncles joined us for more festivities and special foods.

As an adult, I duplicated many of these traditions with my own family. I couldn't imagine ever missing any of the holiday's significant events, thinking the absence would be difficult for all. But when our fourth child arrived on her due date of December 25th in Paris, we experienced a unique and wonderful Christmas.

For those suffering abuse and exploitation at Christmas and every day, I'm donating my anthology proceeds to the International Justice Mission (ijm.org).

About Janet

Janet Joanou Weiner grew up in southern California and studied French against her sixth-grade teacher's advice that she'd never use it. Janet has now lived in France for over two decades—first in the Alps, then in the center of Paris for several wonderful years. Currently, she resides with her husband in St. Hippolyte du Fort in southern France, where they have established a Christian training center, YWAM Bridges of Life.

For her work in Christian ministry, Janet has had the joy of traveling to over forty countries. She's also lived in Amsterdam, the San Francisco Bay Area, and Kona, Hawaii. Despite presently missing her four children and grandchildren, all in the United States, Janet loves her life. She delights in the endless opportunities it affords to discover inspiring stories of a region's past while soaking up its beauty, culture, and history.

Janet dabbled in writing but never found the time to pen a novel until after a significant birthday, when she decided it was now or never. The historical novels in her Huguenot Resistance Series are based on actual events and take place in her village and even in her home, the 500-year-old Château de Planque.

Enjoy Janet's blog, *Fig & Vine*, at janetjoanouweiner.com.

Recipes

Tender Crisp Sugar Cookies

Nancy Ness

MAKES ABOUT 4 DOZEN COOKIES

Ingredients

1/2 cup butter

1/2 cup shortening

1/2 cup granulated sugar for recipe + 1/4 cup in a bowl for pressing or cutting dough

1/2 cup powdered sugar

1 egg

1 1/2 teaspoons vanilla

2 1/4 cups flour

1/2 teaspoon soda

1/2 teaspoon cream of tartar

1/2 teaspoon salt

Directions

Cream the butter, shortening, and sugars together until fluffy. Beat in the egg and vanilla.

Sift the remaining, dry ingredients together and add to the creamed mixture.

Shape the dough into 1-inch balls and use the bottom of a water glass dipped in water and then granulated sugar to press the balls flat, about 1 inch apart on an ungreased cookie sheet. Or roll out the dough on a lightly floured surface and use a cookie cutter dipped in water and sugar.

Bake in a 375-degree oven for 10–12 minutes. Cool on a rack.

About This Recipe

My nana's "best sugar cookie recipe ever" has been handed down through three generations of my family. I use it to bake cookies with my daughters and granddaughters every Christmas.

Rohlicky

Sarah Soon

MAKES ABOUT 80 PASTRIES

Dough Ingredients
2 packages dry yeast
1/2 cup warm water
2 teaspoons sugar
1 pound margarine (4 sticks)
4 cups all-purpose flour
4 egg yolks, separated

Directions
Combine the warm water with the yeast and sugar. Cover and let rise while making the dough.

Mix the margarine and flour as for pie crust. Add the beaten egg yolks and mix well. Add the yeast mixture and blend well. The dough will be sticky.

Make small balls the size of walnuts. Place them on a cookie sheet and refrigerate them for at least 3 hours (best overnight), until thoroughly chilled.

Filling and Baking Ingredients
2 cups ground nutmeats (I use walnuts)
1 1/2 cups granulated sugar
4 stiffly beaten egg whites
3 tablespoons melted butter
1 tablespoon vanilla
3 cups powdered sugar (for rolling and dusting)

Directions
Mix all but the powdered sugar well, to a smooth paste.

On a surface sprinkled with powdered sugar, roll out each dough ball into a flat circular shape. Place 2 teaspoons of filling across the middle of the circle and loosely roll up the dough so it resembles a croissant. Seal edges slightly. Place the rohlicky logs on a slightly greased cookie sheet, and then carefully curve edges so they resemble a half-moon. Make sure the sides are sealed so the filling doesn't come out during baking.

Bake until very lightly browned, about 12–15 minutes at 350 degrees. Let them cool for a few minutes after baking, then place them carefully on a cooling rack. You can sprinkle the rohlicky with powdered sugar now or when ready to serve them.

About This Recipe
Rohlicky is a Czech pastry my grandma learned to make from her mom, who emigrated to the United States from Czechoslovakia. My grandma made them every time we'd visit her in the summer, so eating these treats became one of the many highlights of my week spent with

my grandparents. Anytime someone in the family bakes these, we not only get excited to devour them but are happy we're keeping the family legacy alive.

Taralle with Almond Buttercream Frosting

Linda Sammaritan

Makes about 100 cookies

Dough Ingredients
1 cup sugar
1/2 pound butter, softened
6 eggs
3 teaspoons vanilla extract
6 cups flour
6 teaspoons baking powder

Directions
Cream the butter and sugar. Add the eggs 2 at a time, stirring in between. Add the vanilla.

Stir in the flour and baking powder. *I start with 2 cups of flour and 2 teaspoons of baking powder, mix that well, and repeat the process until all dry ingredients form a stiff dough.* The last 2 cups of flour will require mixing with your hands. No spoon has been strong enough. So start with extremely clean hands!

Cover the bowl of dough with plastic wrap or a lid and leave it in the refrigerator overnight.

Each cookie is shaped individually. Pinch off a ball of dough about 1 inch across. Roll it on a clean counter until it's the size of a pencil—about 8 inches long. Take the ends of the "pencil" and flip it into a bowknot. *My mother-in-law could do this in a fraction of a second with the dough in midair! I keep mine on the counter and tie a bowknot.*

Bake on an ungreased cookie sheet at 350 degrees for 10–12 minutes. The cookies will be golden brown on the bottom.

Remove cookies to foil or waxed paper and allow to cool completely before frosting.

Frosting Ingredients
2 sticks (1 cup) butter, softened
4 cups sifted confectioners' sugar
2 tablespoons milk
1 teaspoon vanilla extract
1 teaspoon almond extract
food coloring as desired

Directions
Cream the butter and sugar. Stir in the milk, vanilla, and almond extract. Add a little water if you want thinner frosting. Add food coloring, if desired, until thoroughly mixed.

With a knife, spread frosting on the top of each cookie, as much or as little as you desire!

When this German girl married into an Italian family, I discovered that my mother-in-law and all of the aunts each had her own "secret ingredient" to make her cookie "the *best*." I eventually included my own secret ingredient, and I'm not saying what that is. But I do know it makes for the *best* taralle!

My sons are all past 40 and behave like disappointed little boys if I don't make taralle for the holidays.

Old-Fashioned Peppermint Mocha Fudge

Mari Eygabroad

Makes about 1 pound

Ingredients

3 cups castor sugar

2/3 cup cacao powder, sifted

1 tablespoon instant coffee granules

1 1/2 teaspoons ground cinnamon

1/2 teaspoon salt

1 cup whole milk or cream

1/2 cup evaporated milk

3 tablespoons unsalted butter

2 teaspoons pure vanilla extract

1/4 teaspoon peppermint extract

Directions

Line a baking sheet or 8-inch square pan with buttered parchment paper or foil and set aside.

In a medium bowl, combine sugar, salt, and cocoa powder. Set aside.

In a small bowl, dissolve the instant coffee and cinnamon in 2 teaspoons of hot water. Stir until a paste forms, and set aside.

In a medium saucepan, combine the whole milk, evaporated milk, and sugar mixture.

Heat over medium heat, stirring constantly with a wooden spoon until the sugar dissolves and the mixture comes to a full boil. *Approximately 15 minutes.*

Reduce heat to medium-low and continue to cook, stirring occasionally until the temperature reaches 234–240 degrees Fahrenheit (112–116 degrees Celsius). *Approximately 30 minutes. Even if you have a candy thermometer available, thermometers may not always be accurate. As the cooking time nears the end, drop some of the mixture into cold water. If a soft ball forms, it is ready. If you would like a firmer fudge, cook a few minutes longer.*

Remove from heat. Add the butter but do not stir.

Allow the mixture to cool in the pot until the butter is melted and the bottom of the pot feels very warm to the touch but not hot. *Approximately 30 minutes.*

Add the vanilla, peppermint, and coffee-cinnamon mixture and beat with a wooden spoon until the mixture loses some of its gloss. *Approximately 6–8 minutes.*

Quickly spread the mixture onto the parchment-lined baking sheet to form a slab of your desired thickness or into the 8-inch square pan for a uniform appearance.

Cool for 2–3 hours (even overnight) at room temperature, before cutting into squares.

Enjoy! Store in an airtight container at room temperature for approximately 2 weeks or in the fridge for 3–4 weeks. You can freeze the whole slab or pieces, well-wrapped and in a double bag, for up to 3 months.

About This Recipe

My mother used to make fudge every Christmas. While this is not the exact recipe my mother used—she used the Fantasy Fudge recipe on the Marshmallow Fluff container—the combination of coffee, peppermint, and chocolate give this fudge a distinct taste. I hope you enjoy it as much as I have.

Cream Puffs

Susan Graham

MAKES 20-30 PUFFS, DEPENDING ON SIZE

Dough Ingredients
2 cups water
1 cup shortening
1/2 teaspoon salt
2 cups all-purpose flour
6–8 eggs

Directions
Bring the water, shortening, and salt to a boil in a pot on the stove.
Stir in the flour till the mixture leaves the sides of the pot.
Place the dough in a bowl and let it cool for 30 minutes.
Add the eggs one at a time, beating the mixture well with a wooden spoon after each.
Heat oven to 450 degrees.

Put rounded teaspoons of dough on an ungreased cookie sheet.

Bake at 450 degrees for 10 minutes, then 400 degrees for 15 minutes. The puffs should be a light golden brown.

Cool and slice the puffs open about halfway and take out any uncooked dough.

Filling Ingredients
2 small boxes vanilla instant pudding
1 pint heavy cream
1 pint milk

Directions
Beat together the pudding, cream, and milk till thick.
Fill the puffs.
Dust the puffs with powdered sugar.
Note: You can replace the vanilla pudding with chocolate and also drizzle the puffs with melted chocolate.

About This Recipe
This recipe came to me through my cousin Loretta and immediately became a family favorite. The first time you prepare it may be a bit of a pain and— Well, you'll see. Trust me.

Gluten-Free Jammed Thumbs

J. Bea Wilson

MAKES ABOUT 2 DOZEN COOKIES

Ingredients

3/4 cup teff flour

2 tablespoons cocoa powder

1/4 teaspoon sea salt

1/4 cup pure maple syrup

1/3 cup unsalted butter, melted

1/2 teaspoon vanilla extract

1/2 cup unsweetened tahini

1/2 cup jam, at room temperature

Preheat oven to 350 degrees and line a 24-inch cookie sheet or two 12-inch sheets with parchment paper. Sift the teff flour, cocoa powder, and sea salt into a small bowl, whisk until well blended, and set aside.

In a medium bowl, whisk together the maple syrup, melted butter, vanilla, and tahini, until well blended. Add the dry ingredients to the wet and mix with a spoon just until blended. Mixture will be oily.

Use a 1-tablespoon scoop or roll the dough into tablespoon-size balls and place them about 1 inch apart on the cookie sheet(s). With slightly damp fingers, smooth any rough spots. This will lessen the cracking of the dough during baking, prevent the cookies from becoming too dry, and polish their appearance.

Bake in the preheated oven for 5 minutes. Pull the cookies from the oven and use a slightly damp thumb to make a well in each cookie for the jam. Fill each well just below its top edge with jam, about 1/4 to 1/2 teaspoon.

Bake in the oven for 10 minutes more. Let the cookies cool on the sheet(s) for a minute or so, then remove them with a spatula to a cooling rack. Allow complete cooling before you enjoy.

A drizzle with thin white icing is one way to dress up these brown cookies. They can be stored at room temperature and are even tastier the next day.

About This Recipe

I created this recipe especially for this anthology, by drawing from a few versions available online and adding my own touches. I'm a fan of recipes that supply nutritional value—in this case, protein and iron.

Shrimp Mold

Janet Joanou Weiner

MAKES APPROXIMATELY 4–5 CUPS

Ingredients
1 10.5-ounce can condensed cream of shrimp soup (can substitute lobster)
8 ounces cream cheese
1 envelope gelatin powder
2 tablespoons milk
1 cup mayonnaise
1 cup thinly chopped celery
1 small can shrimp, drained
4 green onions, chopped (tops too)

Directions
Heat the soup and cream cheese in a large pan over low heat.

Mix the gelatin with the milk and add to the soup mixture. Stir until dissolved.

Add in the rest of ingredients.

Pour the mixture into a 5-cup mold (I use a fish-shaped one) and cover with plastic wrap. Refrigerate to firm.

Tips for removing the dip from the mold: Remove at least 30 minutes before serving time. Place the mold with the dip side down on a flat serving plate. A hot towel on the outside of the mold can help loosen it. Also, running a knife between the edge of the dip and the mold can help separate them.

Fresh dill or parsley makes a nice garnish. If you use a fish-shaped mold, serve with a thin slice of pimento-stuffed green olive for an eye.

This dip is delicious with buttery wafer crackers or thin bread slices.

Enjoy!

About This Recipe

Once my mom discovered this Shrimp mold, no Christmas Day in our home would be complete without it. When I married, she gave me a fish-shaped copper mold, which I still use every year. I hope you enjoy this creamy, slightly decadent dip as much as my family does.

Bea-Linda-Mari-
Lady
Lits
Nancy-Sarah-Susan-